Three b................................... ....forever.

A charismatic trio of brokers have built a billion-dollar empire buying, selling and discovering new artworks. Their dashing good looks and smooth-talking charm have even earned them a TV show and their own on-screen personalities: Krew is The Brain, a sharp intellect and a wiz at auction. Joss is The Brawn, a gorgeous thrill seeker with muscles to match. And Asher is The Face, a handsome devil who can charm his way into any art deal.

But in the high-stakes art world, where everything could be lost in an instant, are any of them willing to risk it all for love?

Find out in

Faking It with The Boss

Billion-Dollar Nights in the Castle

Jet-Set Nights with Her Enemy

All available now!

Dear Reader,

This is the final story in my trilogy about The Art Guys and their billion-dollar lifestyle. I love writing in a miniseries because it gives me an opportunity to continue to follow secondary characters and really dive into their world. Of course, there are some cameos from *Faking It with Her Boss* and *Billion-Dollar Nights in the Castle*. And there's a short read also included in the series, *Tryst with a Trillionaire*, which is an online read that you can find on the Harlequin and Mills & Boon websites.

I love all the arts and like to incorporate my favorites onto the page. So of course my heroes' and heroines' favorites will be the same as mine. The Mucha Museum in Prague is on my wish list!

I hope you enjoy reading Krew and Peachy's story!

Michele

JET-SET NIGHTS
WITH HER ENEMY

MICHELE RENAE

 **Harlequin**
ROMANCE

Harlequin®
ROMANCE

ISBN-13: 978-1-335-47052-2

Jet-Set Nights with Her Enemy

Copyright © 2025 by Michele Hauf

Recycling programs for this product may not exist in your area.

Harlequin Enterprises ULC
22 Adelaide St. West, 41st Floor
Toronto, Ontario M5H 4E3, Canada
www.Harlequin.com

Printed in U.S.A.

Michele Renae is the pseudonym for award-winning author Michele Hauf. She has published over ninety novels in historical, paranormal, and contemporary romance and fantasy, as well as written action/adventure as Alex Archer. Instead of "writing what she knows," she prefers to write "what she would love to know and do" (and yes, that includes being a jewel thief and/or a brain surgeon).

You can email Michele at toastfaery@gmail.com.
Instagram: @MicheleHauf
Pinterest: @ToastFaery

Books by Michele Renae

Harlequin Romance

A White Christmas in Whistler

Their Midnight Mistletoe Kiss

Art of Being a Billionaire

Faking It with the Boss
Billion-Dollar Nights in the Castle

Fairy Tales in Maine

Cinderella's One-Night Surprise

If the Fairy Tale Fits...

Cinderella's Billion-Dollar Invitation

Cinderella's Second Chance in Paris
The CEO and the Single Dad
Parisian Escape with the Billionaire
Consequence of Their Parisian Night
Two Week Temptation in Paradise

Visit the Author Profile page at Harlequin.com.

CHAPTER ONE

NUMBER 8. HER LUCKY NUMBER. Peachy Cohen set the auction paddle on the empty folding chair beside her. Before her on stage, the Van Marks' Auction House manager oversaw the white-gloved crew bringing out the next painting to place on the block. Titled *Melancholy*, by French painter George Devereux, it had just been released from a private collection. It depicted a ghostly white Victorian-period woman sitting before a pianoforte while her startled and bereaved husband watched her create a haunting melody from the shadows.

It was this painting Peachy was here to bid on. And win.

Picking up her purse from the floor beside where she'd laid her cane, she ran her fingers over the Hermès silk scarf she kept tied to the handle—a good-luck talisman—then sorted through it in between glances at the competition in the seats around her. The usual suspects were bidding this afternoon in this subdued London salesroom. All of them men, save the one elderly woman in the back, her silver hair swept up in a stylish chignon and her choice in brick-red lipstick spot-on.

Peachy's employer at the Hammerstill Gallery—the notoriously grumpy Heinrich Hammerstill himself—had given her a want list of four paintings to win and bring back to the gallery. Each would be auctioned separately at various auction houses. None must end up in someone else's hands. Today's lot was the first of the four.

Pulling out her compact, she checked her makeup. Her lipstick needed a bit of retouching, so she pulled out a bold red lipstick and dabbed her lips. In the mirror, she took in those seated behind her. Silver chignon stood, preparing to leave. There were only two items remaining for bid. Many had already left the sales floor.

But there. Panic squeezed her heart. She hadn't noticed *him* earlier when assessing the room for competition. Must have walked in late. Or, more specifically, arrived just in time for the item he sought.

Peachy snapped her compact shut and set her purse on the floor. She'd swear, but that was no way to maintain her composure.

Krew Lawrence sat two rows behind her on the opposite side of the aisle. The man was a reality television personality, dubbed The Brain for his smarts and art knowledge. Lawrence was a shark at auction. Rarely did he lose a bid. He was one of three men who owned the London-based billion-dollar art brokerage The Art Guys. They were celebrities in the art world.

And where those men went…

With a surreptitious glance over her shoulder she spied the two-man film crew at the back of the room. Media were not allowed onto the sales floor, but apparently a television show had some clout. They had stationed themselves behind the last row of empty chairs. One held the camera, obviously filming. The other held a shotgun mic.

Smoothing a hand across her tightening stomach, Peachy blew out a calming breath. The Brain couldn't possibly have an interest in the painting she was here to win. But just in case…

She crossed her legs slowly, one hand slipping unobtrusively along her thigh to slightly inch up her red-and-white polka-dot skirt. A careful glide of her leg along the other should draw attention to the black patent-leather shoes that did not have a high heel but the straps gave them a sexy allure. This position was always taxing to her hip, which she'd injured years ago, but she would maintain it for the sake of her win.

With a calculated bow of her head, she twisted it to look over her shoulder. Lowered her lashes. Parted her lips…

Mr. Lawrence looked up from his phone. Directly at her. Mercy, he was handsome. Dark hair cut short on the sides and left a little longer on top emphasized his square face, and the trim beard further framed his handsome features, his straight nose. The telly did no justice to his shimmering green eyes or even that tiny mole above his eyebrow that danced as he frowned. He gave a tilt of his head as he studied her. *Surveyed* her.

She opened her mouth slightly. Jutted her chin. And then, crossing her fingers beneath the auction paddle, she turned to face the stage where the auctioneer detailed the provenance of *Melancholy.*

Had that sultry yet coy look been meant for him?

Krew noted the initial bid. A lowball. He never tossed out the first bid, knowing it was always wisest to first discern his competition. The auctioneer sought the next bidder and found it in the front row. Then another bidder. And then *she* lifted her paddle.

She wasn't going to win. And those sexy legs weren't going to help her either. He was impervious to female flirtation.

With a nod of his head, Krew bid. Everyone had their bid style and the auctioneers at all the

London houses were aware of his method. He couldn't be pressed to lift a paddle.

As the auctioneer sought another bid, Krew's eyes strolled along those long legs a second time. Sleek and bare, impossibly tantalizing. The shoes had thin black straps that crissed and crossed up her ankles. Caged in soft leather and tied as if a gift.

Krew's heart performed a sort of jump. Very odd.

The inner stutter alerted him to the auctioneer's prompt. Right. *Pay attention, Lawrence.*

He nodded to make another bid. Glanced to the film crew now standing to the side of the main floor. They were recording everything. And he was equipped with a lavalier mic pinned to his suitcoat lapel. Much as the television series "increased their socials," as The Art Guys' receptionist Maeve was wont to gush, he didn't care for the filming process. At least, not this banal, everyday kind of stuff. Nor did it please him that he was not allowed to direct or edit the content the crew captured. But Joss and Asher, his business partners, found great value in the show so who was he to argue the inconvenience of being followed 24/7?

This oil on canvas was lovely. Painted by a late-nineteenth-century French artist whose most popular works had been book illustrations, the majority of the canvas was dark, utilizing blacks, browns and deep umbers for mood, save for the brilliant creamy white tones of the female spirit seated before a very much alive and grieving man who had lost his wife. It was haunting. But not to Krew's taste.

It didn't matter that he cared little for the work. Krew needed to acquire this painting for a client: his father, Byron Lawrence. The Lawrence family was old money, and old art. Lots of both. To the point that if a family member did not admire art then a DNA test was suggested, not even facetiously. Krew's father had amassed an immense collection over his lifetime. It was an obsession. A vulgar display of wealth. But Krew would never suggest that to Byron, who measured his son's value by his bank statement and his ability to bring him yet another rare artwork.

Since forming The Art Guys eight years ago, Krew had helped Byron to procure a Rembrandt, a da Vinci and a Caravaggio.

The old man had divorced last year. For the third time. And his ex-wife, a Frenchwoman, had made off with some of Byron's prized pieces when she'd been clearing her things out of his home. Now Claudia was selling them, knowing it would drive her ex crazy. And she wasn't selling them all at the same auction house. Nor was she releasing info on the sales until a day or two beforehand. It was clear she wanted Byron to suffer the loss of the paintings slowly.

Krew had initially balked at being drawn into his dad's marital vendetta. But when Byron had pointed out the similarities between his third marriage and Krew's own brief marriage, Krew had agreed that a calculating woman should not be allowed victory after ruining a man's life so thoroughly.

His own marriage… Well, mistakes had been made.

So here he sat, his father's son in every aspect. Entitled art aficionado. Lonely heart. Unworthy of a real, true love. Eager to set the scales of justice to balance.

Thinking those descriptions of his father—and de facto, *him*—made Krew shake his head. Was he really such a pitiful case? No. He wasn't entitled, nor lonely. He had quite a good life. His work with The Art Guys made him happy. As for love? It wasn't that he felt unworthy of it, only… He wondered, was he even *capable* of true intimacy? He wanted love. He just wasn't sure how love actually worked emotionally. He'd never had a decent role model for it.

As his ears followed the exchange of bids, Krew's eyes again strayed to the slide of long, graceful fingers along thigh. That was a move a man should make, lingering on the softness of her skin, exploring the trek upward to that curvaceous—

The woman glanced his way. Krew narrowed his gaze. Something about her seemed familiar. That dress—red with white polka dots—hugged her every curve jealously. He didn't know her personally, but he was aware she was a dealer with a local gallery owned by Heinrich Hammerstill. Not The Art Guys' favorite dealer in London.

She didn't so much smile as make him a promise in the lush purse of her reddest-of-red lips. That promise tightened about Krew's heart, but nothing could storm the rampart into the tender center of a heart that, once broken, had pulled up armor.

Turning her attention back to the stage, a subtle shake of her head sifted her wavy charcoal hair in a sway. It wasn't long enough to reach her shoulders, and exposed a pale, swanlike neck.

With the bang of the auctioneer's hammer, the bidding came to an end.

Krew shook himself out of his observation of the woman.

Wait. Had he won?

Gentle applause accompanied the auctioneer's announcement that Miss Cohen of the Hammerstill Gallery had won the Devereux.

Krew's jaw dropped open. He never lost a bid. And those in the business knew it.

He huffed and moved to adjust his lapel in frustration, then caught himself. If he placed a hand over the microphone he wore the crew would complain at the feedback.

With a graceful glide to stand, the woman picked up her purse and turned to walk down the aisle. She was as steady as a gazelle gliding down the runway despite the fact she used a cane. She didn't lean on it heavily, as if she didn't actually need it for support. Curious.

Just as they came parallel, she winked at him. A triumphant smile followed along with a tilt of her head. An aura of crisp citrus perfume and sensuality sashayed along with her. So familiar...

Krew clutched his hands into fists. It felt as though he'd just been swept by a hurricane. This was bad form.

The man sitting beside him leaned in and muttered, "Tough luck, Mr. Brain. Don't take it so hard. She's a honeypot. That woman could have us all with a wink. Too bad she's broken."

Annoyed at the man's crass label, Krew countered, "You are the broken one, sir, to imply any human could be such a thing."

The old man huffed and crossed his arms over his chest.

Krew turned to look down the aisle, more as a means to distance himself from the rude comment. The woman had exited the room. The camera crew, now repositioned near the door, had obviously caught that sensual glide of triumph past her defeated opponent.

Krew had just...failed.

And the film crew had recorded it all.

CHAPTER TWO

TWO DAYS LATER Krew stood before his mirror, tying a Windsor knot in his purple silk tie. A knot that instilled feelings of success. After the lost bid the other day he needed it. But just the thought that he needed some sort of token or magical knot to aid his luck today disturbed him.

He was a confident man. Hell, confidence was 75 percent of the game. The other 25 percent was knowledge. Things always went his way. And if they didn't? He could generally buy his way into or out of whatever the situation demanded. But he never used money as a tool, lure or even bribe. He'd leave that to his father. Krew simply knew the art world well and had honed his skills at auctions and appraising. Not to mention he was an expert at spotting a forgery. Those skills gave him clout others respected.

He'd lost the *Melancholy* painting to Peachy Cohen. His reflection wrinkled a brow. What kind of name was Peachy? Was it even a real name? It alluded to sweet things and a sensual appeal. Which the woman had. In spades. He didn't want to admit it to himself, but he'd been distracted by her during the auction. She had been the reason he'd lost.

An irritating admission, as Krew Lawrence was not the type to be distracted by a sexy woman. He preferred his women more astute and even bookish. A woman who enjoyed numbers and finances, as well as being versed in the arts. It was Byron whose girlfriends and wives had been obsessed with celebrity sightings and fashion. Sexy on the outside, vapid on the inside. They didn't know art. And if pressed, they'd bring up artist names that he considered entry-level.

With a wince, he checked himself. How quickly he slipped into "Byron mode." Krew tried never to judge a person by their outer appearance and knew it was unfair of him to do so. Besides, he certainly would never place his mother in the same category as that cruel assessment of his father's past loves. Despite her moving out of his life when he was six, they still spoke once a month. She was the one who taught him there was much more beneath the skin, embedded in the very DNA of a person, that made every one of them a marvel. And thanks to his work with the public—through galleries, art events and charity soirees—he met many interesting characters and had expanded his knowledge of human nature beyond the Lawrence family's paternal legacy of "money equals power."

But such knowledge had not helped him avoid distraction at the auction.

Marvelous was the first word that came to mind to describe Miss Cohen. Followed closely by *dangerous*. Especially to a man who had difficulty knowing how to act around women, leery of making a wrong move thanks to his experience with his ex-wife, Lisa.

The last thing he wanted was to follow his old man's steps and go for wife number two. Byron collected women without a care; they were as much a prize to him as a Rembrandt or a Michelangelo. Yet at least Byron—he preferred Krew address him by his first name and not the sappy Dad or Father—was able to let go of the women. Not that he had a choice. They generally fled him. Along with a sizable settlement.

No, Krew would not follow Byron's lothario footsteps. He was done with relationships that might break a man's heart. His was tattered but the armor he'd pulled around it kept it functional. Though hookups were not his thing either. When a man had sex with a woman it had to be meaningful. He wasn't about to waste himself on surface attractions and one-night stands.

He tugged the tie knot to perfection. A Windsor was classic. Like Scottish whisky in a fine crystal decanter. Italian leather loafers. And a 1960s Aston Martin with the top down while cruising the countryside. Thinking of which, he really needed to get that out for a drive in the country.

Normally, he'd mark his rare loss as a bump on the road, but unfortunately, he could not. Krew had promised Byron he'd bring back all four paintings to fill those bare spots on the wall of the Lawrence estate. It was a matter of manly pride. Claudia must not be allowed to humiliate Byron in such a manner.

And Krew might finally get a sort of vicarious emotional closure for the cruel words Lisa had flung at him after she'd walked out of their divorce proceedings.

He hadn't been there for her emotionally? Well. That was neither here nor there now. So, onward.

The paintings on his list had originally been purchased by Byron through the Hammerstill Gallery over a period of a year. The Art Guys had just been getting started so they had been some of Byron's last purchases that hadn't gone through his son.

"Hammerstill," Krew growled at his reflection.

Why could The Art Guys not distance themselves from the Hammerstill Gallery? They'd never had a pleasant interaction with the man or his associates. Asher, one of Krew's partners at the brokerage, had last year gone toe to toe with the bombastic owner, Heinrich Hammerstill, over representing a prospective artist. Both had lost, and the artist had ultimately insisted on representation by their The Art Guys' talented receptionist, Maeve. That was a different story entirely.

The loss of *Melancholy* had cracked Krew's perfect record, but he was far from mortally wounded.

Three paintings remained on Byron's list and Krew had a spy in his pocket. Maeve, who was currently transitioning from full-time receptionist to a few days a week because she also owned a decor shop in the West End, had a flatmate, Lucy, who was related to Byron's ex-wife Claudia. Lucy Ellis was familiar to Krew as she'd recently become engaged to one of his most philanthropic clients, Conor Gavin. Lucy apparently wasn't close with Claudia, but she was following her on her private social channels, so he had an in to tracking the paintings.

The first auction had been a fluke. Miss Cohen couldn't possibly be at the one today. And if she were? He'd focus his attention on the auction block as if wearing blinkers. He had never let something so superficial as a pretty smile and sexy legs interfere in business before, and he wouldn't begin making a habit of it now.

And he had to remember these auctions were being filmed for an episode of The Art Guys. Any more mistakes would be recorded for the world to see, and that prospect was unacceptable to Krew. The last thing he needed was to be seen to fail so publicly. His father would never let him forget it.

Peachy adjusted the silk scarf tied on her purse strap as she waited for bidding to begin on the next lot. Mr. Lawrence was here again today, and looking delicious in a tailored suit that emphasized his straight shoulders and perfect posture. She had a photo of him on her vision board at home. He inspired her in so many ways. But never had she thought he'd be so devastatingly handsome in person. It was hard to suppress her blush at the thoughts that ran through her head around that man.

He hadn't bid on the previous six items. If he bid on the next painting she'd have to start becoming suspicious of his motives.

The canvases she sought were by different artists, painted in various time periods and styles, and were being sold at different auction houses. The only thing that tied them together was the seller, who had just released them after years of ownership.

Heinrich Hammerstill had taken a step away from auctions and even the sales floor over the past year, which was why she'd been sent to bid on the paintings instead. The man was in his seventies and age was not treating him fairly. He had breathing issues, took medications and was moodier than his usual grumpy self. Peachy sensed he would soon completely step away from the gallery, which could mean a move up to gallery manager for her. She had no designs on living in London permanently, but the increase in salary would mean an increase in the savings she had earmarked for a home of her own. She was so over her tiny studio flat in Mayfair. She wanted the independence of being a homeowner, with the stability and peace it would provide. Two things she'd never experienced growing up in her bohemian mother's household.

The Devereux painting Peachy had won the other day was now safely stored in a holding site away from the gallery, and Peachy and Heinrich were the only two who had access to it.

The hammer pounded and the audience jumped. Peachy looked to the stage. Krew Lawrence sat in the second row from the front, two rows ahead of her. Again he was on the aisle seat. He hadn't noticed her. Yet.

She needed to focus, and pray The Art Guys' budget for the piece was smaller than her own. The thought turned her stomach. The Art Guys was a billion-dollar enterprise. Those men had money, and the three of them were skilled, knowledgeable, charming and confident. Literal geniuses who had combined their expertise, they seemed to hold the world in their hands. And art was their forte.

The auctioneer briefly introduced the painting. *The Deluge* by Mongline, a painter known for his illustrations inspired by the Bible and literature, featured a Greek god holding his wife aloft as floodwaters swirled around them. Peachy liked the message that the man would risk his own life to save his wife's. So romantic. Also, the light in the work was ethereal. And, okay, there was also the fact that the man's muscles were nothing to sneeze at. Peachy would never say no to being hoisted over his shoulders!

The hammer pounded the block and she gripped her bidding paddle. *Time to bring home muscles.*

A handful of bidders thrust up their paddles, while others tugged an ear or winked as their bidding technique. The price rose quickly and Mr. Lawrence eventually tossed in his nod.

Peachy did have a bidding cap, but she'd spent less than expected on *Melancholy*, so when the bid exceeded that cap, she took a chance, factoring in the additional 20 percent the auction house added to the hammer price to cover their fees.

Someone coughed, startling her. She twisted to look over the crowd, for the first time noticing the camera crew. What was so interesting about an auction? Of all the episodes she had seen of The Art Guys on the telly, no time had been devoted to the boring auction floor. And she personally preferred the episodes that featured the one known as The Brawn where he traveled to exotic locations and did some wild adventuring to obtain rare artworks. Sure, he was a stud, but the location scenes were always the main draw for her.

Alerted by the auctioneer's voice, Peachy shifted out of her wandering thoughts and turned to raise her paddle. Mr. Lawrence twisted a look over his shoulder—that tiny freckle above his eye wiggled with an arch of his brow—then matched her bid. Another look from him. She winked. Lifted her paddle.

The Brain's eyes were so green. They reminded her of one of her favorite paintings…

The hammer banged the block with finality, closing the sale. Who had won? She'd seemingly bid last, yet she couldn't be sure Lawrence hadn't slipped in another nod to bid.

The auctioneer, with a wry twist of his mouth,

nodded to her and announced she was the winning bidder.

Yes! She'd— Well, she wasn't sure how she'd won that one, but she wasn't going to argue. Or stick around. Even before the painting was lifted from the easel, Peachy rose and exited the salesroom, noting the camera lens followed her every step.

Stopping at the manager's desk outside the sales floor, she confirmed her gallery information and the address the painting was to be shipped to. As she waited for a receipt she spied Mr. Lawrence exiting the auction room. He wasn't staying for the Koons that was scheduled to be the final lot of the afternoon? A big-money dealer like him? Interesting. Surely he couldn't have only been interested in *The Deluge*? It had gone for less than a hundred thousand.

He glanced her way, did a double take, then with a smooth of his tie, lowered his head in a nod of acknowledgment and stuffed his hands in his trouser pockets, seemingly happy to wait for her to come to him.

She told herself it was just a strange coincidence that they'd bid on the same paintings twice in a period of three days. But she also wondered if he might be interested in the next two paintings on her list as well. It seemed unlikely. But she needed to know for sure.

Feeling in control, Peachy squared her shoulders and strolled over to meet him at the heavy brass exit doors where he'd paused.

Fully aware the camera crew lingered but ten meters from Mr. Lawrence, she kept her back to them.

The man must be crestfallen to have lost a bid—twice—given he was famous for his auction wins. But she also knew there was an opportunity here to gain his trust and find out why he was after the exact same paintings she was.

"Winner buys dinner?" she suggested lightly.

Mr. Lawrence turned to her, a sour look on his face. Such expressive brows. And that single freckle above the one that seemed to dance a protest to her standing so close to him. A girlish shiver rippled over her skin. Never had she dared to approach a cute guy in school. Even now, she usually relied on friends to set her up on dates. Standing up to a handsome and obviously smart man like Mr. Lawrence was new territory for her.

He glanced around the lobby as though checking to see no one witnessed their conversation and the camera was no longer rolling. The film crew had already captured the details of his loss in the auction room and it appeared he wasn't keen to give them more entertainment.

"I'd like to buy you dinner, Mr. Lawrence."

She almost said, *as a consolation*, but checked herself. Dashing a finger along her ear to sweep the hair away from her cheek, she tugged in her lower lip. A subtle move that attracted his gaze.

What are you doing? Flirting with the sexiest man alive?

"I, uh…" His gaze fell onto her mouth. A wince said he was feeling badly about the loss. "Yes," he said decisively, giving a tug to his tie. She did favor a Windsor knot, utilitarian as it was. "We should talk."

That sounded more businesslike and let-me-find-out-your-intentions than the friendly consolation meal she'd intended, but it was always best to keep one's enemies close. If he were indeed the enemy.

Peachy looked forward to sitting across the table from the man whose green eyes reminded her of the vivid glowing soul in *The Death of the Gravedigger* by Carlos Schwabe.

"Let's go to the bistro across the street," she suggested, and walked out ahead of him, confident he would follow.

CHAPTER THREE

KREW DID NOT want to share a meal with the woman who had stolen the painting from him. Okay, she hadn't *stolen* it, but…well…she'd been using those long legs and a flutter of her lashes to distract him. Even sitting *behind* him, she had been a distraction. And then someone had coughed and he'd looked away from the stage for a moment and…

Really? Was he going with that feeble excuse? He wasn't a pushover. And yes, he did want to dine with her. Because he wanted to delve beneath the surface of Peachy Cohen. Explore her intricate brushstrokes and movement as if assessing a canvas. How else to truly discern her motives?

Following the waiter to a table, his eyes drifted to Peachy's curvaceous backside. Definitely some movement there. She wore polka dots again, this time white set against a deep blue fabric. Ruffles at her half sleeves and around the hem provided a kind of tease, tempting one to study all the curves they caressed. And why did she seem so familiar to him?

With a clear of his throat, Krew looked beyond the woman to the table, trying to focus his thoughts. One slip and he'd not claim a single painting on his list. That was, if she were after the same ones as he was. Two of them so far did indicate that she may have a list similar to his. Incredible. And strange. Agreeing to dine with her would at least give him a chance to try to decipher his opponent's next likely move.

They ordered wine and once she'd ordered her main she reminded him, "I'm buying, remember?"

Indeed? *Rub it in deeper, lady.* Krew skimmed his gaze over the menu, pausing on the most expensive item he could find. "The filet mignon."

The waiter left them with a carafe of water that glinted in the streetlights that shone through the window. It was midafternoon, yet the mizzle had settled, that London mix of mist and drizzle, turning the sky a brownish gray.

"A Windsor knot," she remarked, her eyes falling to his throat.

Krew straightened. Most would know the common knot.

"It's very professional," she offered. "But perhaps you should have opted for something a little more powerful today. A Trinity or Pratt?"

The woman evidently knew her knots. And she was right; the Pratt would certainly have proven more of a power booster. He should have gone with that one.

"Interesting suggestion, coming from the enemy," he muttered tightly.

"I won fair and square, Mr. Lawrence. Perhaps you got a kink in your neck and your bidding nod was off?"

Even more audacious. But also a little funny.

"You seem quite put off to be sitting across the table from me," she added. She pushed the button on her cane to retract it down to one-third its size and set it on the seat beside her. "I didn't force you here."

"I never pass up a free meal."

Her smile was so lush and confident. Red lips he could dream about for days. "I don't believe that for a minute. So what convinced you to agree? Are curious about me?"

"Hardly—" He caught himself. It wasn't like him to be so defensive. And he couldn't afford to start on the wrong foot if he were to glean any useful information from her. "Very well, I am a trifle curious. You're with Heinrich's gallery?"

"You know that, darling." She sipped the water. "Ask me something interesting."

Really? Like why was it he had difficulty maintaining a stoic facade when something so infinitesimal as the way her tongue collected a water droplet from the edge of the glass could stir his attention at a primal level?

Krew tugged at his tie. "May I ask about the cane?"

"Of course. I was injured years ago. It required a few surgeries to fix my hip. But I retained a middle-ear injury that messes with my balance. I can't make any fast turns or dashes because my proprioception is dodgy. The cane is for support, though I can walk fine, if a little slower, without it."

"I had noticed you possess a remarkable awareness of your— Well." He cleared his throat. If she only knew how he'd already mapped her curves... "The cane does not distract from your beauty."

She lowered her gaze. Blushing? Delicious.

But he was here for more than simple flirtation. "What's your interest in *The Deluge*? And for that matter, *Melancholy*."

"I have no interest."

He quirked a brow.

"I obtained the works for the gallery. And don't ask what my boss's interest is. Heinrich maintains a quirky collection. I know you're familiar with it."

"You do?"

"It wouldn't be wise for The Art Guys to not

be familiar with all the local galleries and auction houses. I've been told you're the man to
go to. The one who knows everything about…
Well…" She smirked. "Word also tells you never
lose an auction."

Krew curled his fingers about the wineglass
just as the waiter arrived to offer refills. The
glide of Peachy's long fingers over the top of her
glass distracted. A slow, tactile summation. He
swallowed and focused on his own glass.

"I wouldn't say *never*. We all have our off
days," he said. "Hammerstill has a list, I take it?"

"Let's not talk about my perfidious boss. I'd
prefer our dinner to be light and friendly. Can
we agree to that?"

He shrugged, agreeing. Anything to keep
her talking. He'd learn what he needed with pa-
tience.

"Tell me about yourself," she said, dipping her
finger in the glass and then swirling it around
the rim. "Why art?"

Was the woman aware that her every movement was a sensual lure? Well, of course. No one
dressed like that and moved like a siren without
knowledge that it would draw every male eye
within visual distance.

It impacted Krew more than he was willing
to admit, but so it would, given he was a details man who noticed more than most thanks

to having grown up in a house filled with art and sculpture. His mother had been his most avid teacher. When she and Byron had divorced, Krew had been a mere six years old. He wished he and his mum were closer, but she now lived in Nebraska on a pig farm. Happy as can be.

Krew looked away from Peachy's glass, and that wet finger. She'd asked why he'd gotten into art. "Why not art? It's a lucrative business."

"One has to have a love for it to make such a fortune as you have, Mr. Lawrence. Or should I call you The Brain?"

"Please don't. It's a silly moniker the show's producers slapped on me." He glanced around the restaurant. The camera crew had not been allowed inside—it was difficult to get permission to film in public places at short notice—so for now he could relax. "I've enjoyed art of any kind since I was little. The walls in our estate were plastered with masterpieces, with barely any room between the frames. I started going to auctions with my dad when I was five, and Mum would quiz me on the masters as we strolled museums. I've never not known and admired art."

"I grew up with an artistic mum myself so I can understand that constant immersion in the arts. I can't imagine another profession…" She looked aside and winced. Krew sensed that had been a lie. But what was it she missed?

Their meals were delivered before he could ask. Peachy had ordered carbonara, which she daintily dug into. Her red nails flashed and a strand of dark hair fell over her lashes and across one eye, which she ignored.

"Where did the name Peachy come from?" Krew asked as a means to stop himself suggesting she push away the hair strand that he focused on like a beacon.

"It's on my birth record."

"That's your *real* name?"

"Of course." She looked up. Blinked at the rogue strand of hair. "You think it odd?"

"It is unique."

"And Krew is not?"

Fair.

Did a girl grow into a name like Peachy? Obviously she had. She embodied the name in her walk, her movements, the coy glances and graceful gestures of her hands. But he reminded himself that beneath the surface she was likely so much more than a pretty face. And the urge to uncover more about her intrigued him while also cautioning him. He couldn't know what he was up against.

"So what's next on your auction list, Peachy?"

She waggled her finger in a chastising manner as she finished a bite of food. "We're not talking business."

"I'd like to know as I apparently need to prep for my next auction if you're going to be there."

"I'm no man's competition."

"Well." She was and she wasn't. She'd already pulled off two successes to his detriment. Had he really lost to her because he'd been distracted by long legs and red lips? His father would never forgive him the idiocy. And at the same time, Byron would laugh and comment how his son was just like his old man.

He was not. Was he?

"What's *your* goal?" she asked, settling back in the booth and eyeing him over her wineglass.

His goal was simple: to obtain the paintings for his dad, clap his hands for a job well done... And, being honest, restore his dented ego by managing to metaphorically rescue his father's manhood/ego. Only then could he be satisfied and move on to the next job.

"Like...a life goal," she clarified. "What is it that motivates you, Mr. Lawrence?"

A deep question. What was her strategy?

"I'll tell you my goal," she said eagerly. "It involves two steps. The first of which is advancing at Hammerstill Gallery." She tapped her red nails against the water glass. The ting sounded as delightful as her voice. "I will be successful," she said, though he wasn't sure if she was telling him or herself.

"And part two?"

"Buying my own home. Maybe even a cottage in the country. I have dreams and they will come true. I even have a vision board. And you're on it!"

"I'm… Really?" He didn't know what to say to that. He had kept a vision board while growing The Art Guys so he knew the value of one but—he was on *her* board?

"You inspire me," she said. "You're talented, smart. So calm and classy."

"You flatter me." Sure, he'd become famous with the show, and he was accustomed to being recognized and even signing autographs. But this woman had been *inspired* by him? He'd not received such a genuine compliment before. "Owning a home is a good, solid goal. And life isn't worth living unless one takes on challenge. How does Heinrich feel about your desire to advance?"

"I've told him I'm interested in taking a larger role in the gallery. He's managed the place for decades, but he's ailing. I worry he hasn't many good years left. He's rarely at the gallery these days."

"Interesting." Krew hadn't been aware of the old man's decline in health. Not a surprise as interactions with Hammerstill were never pleasant and Krew tried to avoid them. The television show had once captured the older man berating Asher, whose moniker for the show was The Face, for being nothing more than a pretty boy. It had humiliated Asher. And Krew didn't take kindly to people bullying or trying to discredit those he cared about.

"So, your goal?" she prompted.

"I think I've achieved my goal of success with The Art Guys," he said.

"There's always something more to achieve. To aspire to."

He shrugged. "At the moment, I'm content."

And not willing to allow her in any further, much as he suspected she was trying to learn more about him than he could about her.

"Well." She wiggled on the seat and finally brushed aside that tantalizing strand of hair. "Then perhaps you have the universal human goal?"

"And what is that?"

"Why, to be loved, of course."

Krew set his utensil down with a clank on the plate. Peachy visibly flinched. He hadn't meant to be so demonstrative.

"You don't want love?" she asked with innocence.

"Been there. Done that. Wouldn't recommend it," he hastily blurted out. And at the same time he tossed his napkin over his plate, finished thoroughly with this intrusive conversation.

The sudden touch of her fingers to his hand startled him. Krew tugged away.

"Darling, you are skittish," she said. "And I've gone too far. Forgive me. I simply want to reassure you that we are not working against one another. You've nothing to fear from me."

Could she read his mind?

"I don't fear…" *Any woman.* Or did he? No, she threatened nothing about his career or manhood. As for his emotional needs… "Well, look, this has been—" not as helpful a conversation as he'd hoped and strangely, touching some rather intimate aspects of him he'd rather not acknowledge "—nice. But I should take off. I've work back at the office. Would you entertain an offer on *The Deluge*?"

"Absolutely not."

"Then I guess this is goodbye."

He stood and when she reached for his hand, he wasn't sure what she was going to do, so when the clasp happened he stared at it. Something electrical zapped at his very bones. It prickled in the best way possible. He'd never felt anything like it. Perhaps it was static from his shoes on the carpeting, he tried to tell himself.

The floor was tiled.

"Thank you, Mr. Lawrence. It's been lovely."

He pulled from her grasp, nodded and bee-lined for the front of the restaurant. There, he paid for the meal before leaving.

Once outside, he stepped close to the building to avoid the mizzle. That woman…annoyed him.

And—he studied his hand, still feeling a little tingly—she intrigued him.

The man was far too reserved for the sexy-television-star vibes he gave off. There was nothing and everything nerdish about him. But that tweed vest and his attempts to remain unfazed by her touches had told her so much. She was a tactile person and always dragged her fingers along the items on store shelves, or hedgerows, or racks of clothing in a shop. She liked to feel. To connect.

And Krew Lawrence was a man she wanted to connect with, even if he was a bit tense, and certainly protective of his true feelings. He didn't recommend love? Had he been hurt in a relationship? Possibly. But one bad experience shouldn't ruin a life. She'd meant it when she'd said love was a universal human desire. A need, even. She desired love. Who wouldn't? She sensed Mr. Lawrence required a tender touch. Or two. There was something very desirable about his stoicism. She'd not sat with such a calm and poised man before. It was very refreshing.

Yet, she mustn't allow herself to even consider them as anything more than rivals. Krew Lawrence represented the sort of man she had never been successful in befriending, let alone going beyond into something intimate. Smart, rich, walking an entirely different social level than her, and always on the lookout for nothing more than arm candy. A woman who would enhance his appeal but never interfere with the professional image he presented. Someone to be there for him in his bed, by his side as a decoration, but lacking her own deep thoughts and self-determination.

Of course, she was judging him harshly. But it came easy enough.

The one boyfriend she'd had in high school—they'd dated for a year—had moved to Australia to become a surfer, leaving her heartbroken but hopeful that she had so much life to live and boys and men to discover. At the time she'd thrown herself into her dance studies so not dating hadn't been an issue.

Yet she hadn't dated again until after her accident. Which had put a new twist on trying to relate to someone when she wielded a cane for balance. She'd found the men interested in her—mostly rich art collectors she met through the gallery—were either only in it for a quickie, or to try out a "wounded" woman. So deflating. Thus, she had no idea how real love actually worked.

Peachy lifted her chin. The move reminded her of what her mother had always said when her daughter was feeling less than able. "Darling, lift your chin. Be proud, or at least fake it. A good fake can get you through so much."

But Peachy was never fake. Thanks to her dancing background she knew how to hold herself, even if a cane was now required for balance. And that made it easier to fit in alongside the old boys' club frequently found at auctions, whose confidence was displayed in their stance. It hadn't been easy in the beginning. Their looks assessing her in seconds. The snide glances of the gentlemen making it clear they thought she belonged behind a cosmetics counter instead of in the high-stakes bidding rooms. Or the confusion they displayed when they could not parse the woman in a fitted dress and killer heels who also used a cane. She'd heard the whispers of *afflicted* and *broken*. That did not put her off. In fact, it fueled her desire to succeed. To prove to them all she belonged in their world.

Much as it tired her sometimes. Since losing dance, she'd had to find a way to feel as in her body as dance had once made her feel. That manifested in her fitted clothing and sexy outward appearance. It was her. And it was not.

Would she ever be able to simply be herself? To not have to compete for a place in this world?

But even if she found the love and acceptance she craved, she knew that once found, it would never stay. Her mother was proof of that. So many men had waltzed in and then just as quickly out of Doris Cohen's life. Peachy wanted more than that. She wanted real love.

Peachy sighed and fussed with the silk scarf. A gift from her mum, it depicted a chorus of heavenly figures against a brilliant blue background. It inspired her and gave her hope, so she always kept it with her.

She suspected she had not seen the last of the indomitable man who wore the label The Brain. That she'd won the two paintings he had bid on clearly bothered him. Of course, it must have chinked his ego. But she would never sell to him. The paintings were now Hammerstill's property.

For now, she had to stay on task. And pack for Prague. Though part of her wished Claudia Milton had accepted the tidy sum for all four paintings Hammerstill had offered. But Claudia had refused, saying she wanted to enjoy seeing them auctioned off individually.

Strange. But people had their foibles.

And Krew Lawrence's foible was knotted in his ties. A tell that she knew she'd best pay close attention to.

CHAPTER FOUR

KREW STROLLED INTO The Art Guys' office in central London and thanked Maeve for the black coffee she handed him. Maeve always seemed to know, to the minute, when he'd walk in the door. Of course, it wasn't exactly difficult given he was always punctual, never landing in the office later than three minutes till the hour.

"I have info on your next auction," Maeve said, while typing away at the computer. Her pregnant belly hugged the edge of the desk and it made Krew smile. He knew how excited Maeve and his best friend, Asher, were to meet their little one. "Give me a few minutes to get everything in order," she added.

"Not a problem."

Hearing laughter echo out of Joss's office surprised Krew. Their resident Brawn didn't usually rise until well after the breakfast hour and if he made it into the office before noon he deserved a gold star.

"What's going on?" he declared to the world at large.

Maeve looked up and seemed to realize she was the only one there to answer. "He bopped in this morning to help Asher authenticate a Grecian urn. Both have been here an hour."

Stunned, Krew veered toward Joss's office. Both men greeted him heartily. Asher sat on the corner of Joss's desk, cracking that trademark charming grin that had earned him the moniker The Face. While Joss beamed at Krew.

Coffee unsipped, Krew cast a wondering gaze between the two men.

"Tell him," Asher said with a proud smile.

Joss, dubbed The Brawn for obvious reasons—Krew could never hope to achieve steel abs and biceps like his friend, even with his thrice-weekly gym visits—gave him a shy smile.

"What's going on? Has the world turned on its head? You two are here before 9:00 a.m. and both seemingly coherent? Asher, you never smile so early in the day."

"Joss has news."

News was always welcome. Had Joss nabbed a new client or artist? With a bounce to his step, Joss performed a shadowboxing move before stopping and with splayed hands announcing grandly, "She said yes!"

That could only mean that Ginny, the sweet

librarian Joss had been traveling the world with on his work adventures, had said yes to marriage. The news was indeed grand.

"Congratulations, mate." Krew went in for a hug, and Joss met him with a firm back slap. Krew was thankful Asher had grabbed the coffee cup from him before it could spill.

"All right! You'll crush my tie." Krew stepped back from his friend.

"I'm getting married," Joss repeated. "To Ginny!"

"I had hoped it would be her and not some random stranger you picked up on the Tube." Krew took his coffee back from Asher. "Pints down at the pub to celebrate?"

"You know it." Joss nodded to Maeve, who entered the office. "What's our day look like, Maeve?"

"You'll have to schedule pints early. Krew leaves this evening for Prague."

Krew wasn't surprised when she announced the flight. She was always one step ahead of the three of them and kept the office running smoothly. She would be sorely missed as she would soon be leaving them to run her decor shop full-time, in addition to embracing motherhood. He doubted he would survive a new receptionist, but he supported her dream to own a business suited to her colorful and generous nature.

And her husband, Asher, wouldn't have it any other way.

"Prague is…?" he prompted.

"According to Lucy, the next painting has been placed for auction at the Arthouse," she said. "Tomorrow afternoon. Two o'clock sharp. I was able to book you a room just a quick stroll away from the auction house, but I wasn't able to get you an advance look. It's already been closed for viewing."

"That's fine. I don't need to see the work. My dad once owned the painting." He recalled the small work had hung in the gaudily decorated living room. Byron had acquired it perhaps eight or nine years ago, around the time The Art Guys was just establishing itself. "It's just a matter of getting it back so the old man can place it back on the wall to cover the unfaded portion of wallpaper revealed after it was taken down."

And restoring the old man's bruised ego.

The piece was a minor work by a seventeenth-century Chinese *shuimohua* artist and it featured a large flower in a jar. Thus the title: *Jar and Flower.* Not usually Krew's style, but he did admire it. His mother had been into the Chinese artists and had decorated their living room in the Asian style with all related artwork relegated there as it was acquired.

"You weren't able to get the first two paintings?" Asher asked.

There was no judgment in his tone, but Krew felt the unspoken assessment in his bones. He'd messed up. He'd lost. To a frustratingly, annoyingly, obstinate, *gorgeous* woman who he had best stop thinking about.

And yet. The way she'd stroked the back of his hand in the restaurant…

But then she'd had the nerve to ask him if he believed in love! Or something about love. No, his goal was not love. Much as he wouldn't shove it away if it dropped in his lap, Krew felt the pursuit of it could only end dismally. The Lawrence men were not meant to have love. They certainly didn't know how to *keep* love. If they'd even had it in the first place.

He shook the memory of Peachy asking him about love from his thoughts. "I have plans to make an offer for those two paintings that the buyer won't refuse. It'll all work out."

"Is that buyer a dealer with the Hammerstill Gallery?" Asher asked with as much vitriol as the name Hammerstill deserved.

"Yes, but it wasn't Heinrich. The old codger sent…" If he said an underling, then he'd be claiming that he had been bested by such. He'd not been bested. He'd simply been distracted.

Twice.

"Is the film crew trailing you for these buys?" Joss asked, saving Krew from having to label Peachy.

Krew nodded. "But I'm sure they'll give up. Probably won't make for good telly."

If he could convince the producers of that then those two lost sales would never be aired. And his ego could breathe a sigh of relief. It was bad enough he couldn't find happiness in his personal life, that he felt as though he were following in Byron's footsteps. Why show the world he was also stumbling in his professional life?

"I was talking to Chuck yesterday about a future show," Joss said. Chuck Granville was their producer. "He mentioned something about the crew being interested in following the woman who bid against you. She's gorgeous, apparently."

So they knew. Krew shrugged. "Just another dealer." But… "They're following her?"

"I think they want to add a salacious angle to this one."

"Mercy." Krew sat in Joss's office chair.

"You all right, mate?" Asher asked. "You lost twice. To the *same* woman. Is there—" he exchanged glances with Joss "—something we should know?"

"You got the hots for this woman?" Joss teased.

"I have no such thing," Krew insisted. "I was simply not on my game." He squeezed his eyelids shut. "No. I can handle this. I won't lose the next one. She won't be there. Why would she be? It was just a fluke that she was at the first two auctions."

On the other hand, if she were there again he would have an opportunity to see her, to talk with her. Take her in like the delicious piece of art she was…

"Uh-huh." Again, Joss and Asher exchanged looks.

And Krew could imagine what those looks meant. He'd shared much the same with each of them on occasion. Brewing a salacious story in their minds. Likely painting a picture of a torrid romance with the woman who had bested him.

"She's not my type," he felt compelled to say.

Joss raised his hands in placation. "Didn't say she was or wasn't. But just for reference, what *was* she like?"

Krew sighed. "I don't know. Beautiful. Attentive. Always…touching things. A soft voice, but powerful. And eyes that…undressed me."

Krew smiled at that one. And then he noticed the stunning silence in the room. When he looked up both men were staring at him with grins on their faces.

Finally, Joss splayed both palms outward. "Not going to touch that one, mate. What about you, Asher?"

"Perhaps we'll be announcing another wedding soon, eh?"

Both men laughed, and Krew, grabbing his coffee, quickly exited, leaving the jolly revelers to revel. They knew nothing.

Or did they?

Being on time wasn't her thing. Peachy had missed the call for first-class boarding and was literally the last person on the plane, having flagged down a transport cart because she could not run.

Blowing strands of hair from her eyes, she navigated to her seat, and when she was about to place her carry-on in the overhead bin, a man tapped her on the shoulder.

"Miss? Might we switch seats? There was a seating mix-up and me and my fiancée—" he pointed to the beautiful blonde sitting in the window seat next to Peachy's assigned seat "—were separated."

"Not a problem at all. Where are you sitting?"

"Up two rows. Let me get your bag for you."

"Thank you!" the fiancée called as Peachy allowed the man to move her bag and cane to a bin closer to the front of the first-class cabin.

Didn't matter where she sat. As long as it was business or first class she would be fine as a flight without free champagne was unendurable.

"Am I being punked?" her seatmate said as she sat next to him.

She turned to find Krew Lawrence looking up at her incredulously and laughed. "Oh, darling, this is truly fate."

"I don't believe in such nonsense," Krew said.

She pretended to be affronted as she sat next to him. "Don't be so disappointed. I'm sure I smell much lovelier than he did."

Krew's jaw pulsed as he considered the suggestion. Then he said, "By measures," and crossed his arms over his chest. "Tell me you're not headed to Prague for the Arthouse auction."

With a wiggle, Peachy made herself comfortable. Before crossing her legs, she slipped off her shoes. "I'm not headed to Prague for the Arthouse auction." She cast him a sweet smile and a wink.

He shook his head. "You're lying."

"I just told you exactly what you wanted to hear. You can't make demands of me and then get upset when I do as requested."

"I'm not upset. I'm just gobsmacked. The co-incidences between us have been remarkable."

"Everything happens for a reason."

"Spare me your woo-woo philosophizing."

"Someone woke up on the wrong side of the bed this morning." He probably needed a shot of green juice, her favorite way to start the day. But nothing could match the kick in the feels she got from looking into his gorgeous green eyes. *Don't go all swooning teenager on him! Remember, he could never be interested in you for...you.* "I won't be a bother. I promise you won't even notice me sitting here."

"That's impossible when you look so—"

She smirked as he cut himself off from saying... What? How did she look to him? Appealing? Pretty? Irresistible? Annoying? She'd take any of them, just so long as *he* noticed her. Because he was a man like no other. She barely knew him but her instincts pleaded for her to stick close. Learn him. And figure out why, for some reason, the universe wanted them to be in close proximity.

"Seems we have the same art interests of late." Which wasn't good for her bottom line despite him being intriguing. Was he after the same ink wash painting as she? What was going on? How could Heinrich's list be the same as Krew's? "Where's the film crew?"

"Already in Prague. Waiting for something..." He gestured futilely before them, seeming to seek the right word.

"Interesting? Exciting? Newsworthy?" she tried.

"Salacious," he spit out.

"Mmm." She wiggled on the seat. "I do love a bit of controversy, especially when it's salacious. Not you?"

"Apparently, thanks to my two failures in London—to a beautiful woman, no less—the producers are trying to put the two of us..."

Another extreme facial expression. He hated speaking it, she could tell. It must drive his astute, nerdy self mad. But he had dropped the word *beautiful*. She'd take that.

"Doesn't matter. I'm going to suggest those auctions be cut from the footage. It's not of interest to the show."

"Oh, I don't know. It does offer a glimpse into something most have never seen. That's always interesting. I would have never thought I'd find myself followed by a film crew simply because I've exchanged a few words with a man called The Brain. Such a lark."

"Did you forget dinner?"

How could she? The man had declared a personal vendetta against love. "You were supposed to allow me to pay for that."

She'd been surprised he'd picked up the bill, but also, not so surprised. The man was a gentleman. And she guessed his wallet was bottomless. Of course, he had also claimed part of her win with that move. Not cool.

"As the winner I wanted to buy you dinner."

"And as I fully intend to win the next one, I thought I'd get one step ahead and treat you."

He tugged at his tie. "The film crew is reading too much into this." He sighed. "It's all about ratings and views. Sexual tension makes for good television."

So the film crew thought that she and Mr. Lawrence had sexual tension? Delicious. Of course, she was attracted to the man who knotted his ties so tightly surely the oxygen supply to his brain was reduced measurably. But keeping him close and amiable would only help her cause. And that was more important than falling for his good looks and gentlemanly manner. She needed to keep him at a distance for the sake of another win, so she had best keep her silly thoughts of how handsome he was and how clear and gemlike his eyes were stashed in a deep dark closet. Distraction could prove her downfall.

On the other hand, a man could be manipulated with a flutter of lashes. A pout of one's lips.

A glide of her naked leg along the other. That much she'd learned from her mother.

"Whatever you do," he said, "just stay away from me when the Daves are filming. We don't want it to appear as if anything untoward is happening."

"Darling, I never do untoward," she said with the slightest tease. "Only toward."

His grimace should tickle her but she didn't want to make him angry. Or frustrate him any more than he already appeared to be. "Who are the Daves?"

"Dave Wilcox and David O'Shaunessy. Cameraman and mic operator. Standard minimal crew when not filming action scenes or high-traffic locations. I call them the Daves."

"Convenient if one has trouble remembering names." Which she did. She generally had to speak to a person and use their name a handful of times before the name fixed to her memory.

"Listen, darling." Peachy touched his arm. He didn't flinch as he had when she'd touched him in the restaurant, but he did keep an eye on her hand. Had he not been touched overmuch? Or maybe he was offended by *her* touch? "You're a dear man. A professional. As am I. I want to obtain a specific painting. I will have it. And no amount of *untoward* will win it for me. So don't you worry. This'll be a fair battle. Promise."

"Assuming we are both aiming for the same one?"

"The ink wash. *Jar and Flower*," she said.

He gave her a look of exasperation. So he *was* intent on the same painting. She didn't want to compete with this man. She wanted to befriend him. To get to know him better. To see if a few more touches could relax him.

"Sorry," she felt the need to say. "But I will have that painting."

The pilot announced they were taking off and to fasten seatbelts. Which would allow them a few hours for that getting-to-know-one-another session. Steeped with tension, as she suspected it would now be.

CHAPTER FIVE

ONCE IN THE AIR, Krew liked to go through his emails, research current sales and check for tips on works that may be going on the block. He maintained a corral of informants that included students, collectors, dealers and gallery managers; they never let him down.

However, as he tapped away on the laptop it seemed he wasn't going to be allowed the personal space to indulge in ignoring the beautiful woman to his right.

He looked down where her fingers rested on the crook of his elbow. Matte bloodred nails. Slender wrist. Soft skin that carried the faintest scent. Citrus? Orange, possibly. No, *tangerine*. Something he wanted to inhale and devour as if a juicy treat.

Krew cleared his throat and gave Peachy a pointed look. Head tilted against the back of the seat, she glanced at him. Long, lush black lashes fluttered over luminous brown eyes. Freckles dotted her high cheekbones and dashed the bridge of her tiny nose. A bit of whimsy to soften the turbo-sensuality that crafted Peachy Cohen into a dangerous opponent.

"Do you mind?" he asked carefully. He knew what the answer was going to be.

"Not at all."

Exactly.

If he were to shrug her off he felt it would be akin to pushing away a kitten. No one did that. Even if the kitten had claws that she intended to whip out when the hammer met the block.

"Aren't the clouds dreamy when looking down on them like this?" she asked.

Krew looked out the window. They flew at twelve thousand meters altitude and the crisp blue sky boasted a few clouds that looked like marshmallows. Something he rarely afforded a moment to notice on the hundreds of flights he'd taken in his lifetime.

"Dreamy," he said in a lackluster tone, and re-focused on the laptop screen. Maybe that would be her clue that he wanted to work undisturbed.

With an inhale for fortitude, her scent over-whelmed his senses. He marveled at the bright orangeness of it. Fresh fruit tingling on his tongue. Unique. Appealing.

Dreamy.

"You said your parents gave you a love for art?" she asked.

"Yes." He tapped away on the keyboard.

"I haven't always loved art. I wanted to be a dancer and I was part of a dance troupe when I was a teenager. What about you?"

"When I was a teen I worked at a gallery." He tried to type a sentence in an open email. "Janitor stuff."

Much to his father's horror. *Lawrence men do not do manual labor! We hire the laborers.* Despite being raised by old-money parents, Krew could never fully support that entitled attitude, so while he attended a private school, his after-school hours had been spent exploring the neighborhoods, meeting others his age and hanging out. Like a normal teenager. He didn't regret the exasperated admonishments from Byron either.

"I made friends with one of the dealers at the gallery where I worked," he provided, reminiscing. "He taught me about fakes and forgeries."

"Oh. Yes, I understand from the show that's your focus."

"I hate that fakes exist. That anyone would try to pass off an artwork for something it is not."

"I find it difficult to accept a lie as well. I've never run across a forgery while working at the gallery."

"That you know of. They are ubiquitous in the art world."

"Yes, unfortunately. But I don't think anyone

has been successful in passing off my favorite artist with a fake."

"And which artist is that?"

"Alphonse Mucha was my first love."

Mucha was a nineteenth-century graphic artist who gained initial fame by designing posters for street advertising.

"He's a bit pedestrian for me, but I give the artist credit for bringing the Art Nouveau movement to a groundswell with clean lines, natural forms and ancient symbolism."

"The *Slav Epic* is intense," she said.

Agreed. The massive twenty-panel collection was a feat that Mucha created depicting his homeland and the strife of the Slavs via a mythological approach. Not at all commercial in nature. Certainly a masterpiece.

One of Peachy's fingernails slinked down his arm toward his wrist. Krew paused, fingers curled on the keyboard. Glanced aside at her big innocent eyes. *Not so innocent.* She was up to something. He almost said, *I have work. Do you not see?* but felt a punishing tug in his gut. *Don't be rude to the kitten, Krew.*

And really, his curiosity could not be ignored.

"Mucha is a mass market advertiser's dream." Closing the laptop, he tucked it aside and turned his back to the window, his body toward hers. "But let's talk da Vinci."

That choice seemed to agree with her as she tugged up one leg and readjusted her position to rest her elbow on the narrow armrest between them. Shoes on the floor, he saw that her bare toes were painted to match her fingernails.

"Yes, such an exquisite creator," she said. "The original Renaissance man. I would have loved to have known him. Do you think he was bisexual?"

Mercy. Why did every topic with her always seem to veer toward romantic interest and physical attraction? The woman would try his every nerve.

But for some reason, Krew decided to toss out his thoughts on the rumors that the Renaissance artist had both male and female lovers. Which eventually led to their discussion of the mechanical inventions the polymath artist had drawn. Items such as the parachute, the helicopter and even solar power could be traced to da Vinci's inventive drawings. They both marveled over his anatomical studies of animals and humans, and agreed that his Roman cartography dazzled. Finally, their conversation strayed to the obvious, his most famous works, the *Mona Lisa* and *The Last Supper*.

It made for invigorating discourse. Da Vinci had been Krew's first love and still was. And as Peachy bantered with his ideas and matched his knowledge on da Vinci, he found himself leaning in closer. Hanging on her every word. She knew about the experimental pigments da Vinci had used, which had suffered the effects of time worse than other paints. And that there was a hidden musical score within *The Last Supper*. Both had heard the melody played.

She also leaned closer to him. Her eyes were so bright. Her hands animated as she talked, and every so often that touch to his wrist or leg. As if she were anchoring herself. It didn't bother him so much as he thought it should.

After all, she could be trying to soften him up in order to win another auction. No, it was simply an off-the-cuff conversation. Perhaps it was her manner. Or he hoped it was. Because he hated to believe that she could be a conniving woman who might have plans to stab him in the heart when opportunity presented.

His wife had done that. He hadn't been the same since.

And yet, he had to take half the blame for the failure of his marriage. Lisa had truly felt as though he had not been there for her, and he wouldn't discount her truths. The emotional side of a relationship was not an easy read for him.

When the pilot announced they'd landed in Prague, Krew straightened his shoulders, realizing he'd leaned forward to bow his head closer to Peachy as they'd chatted. Their conversation ended and he felt…disappointed.

Peachy sprang up and grabbed her bag from the overhead bin. "Have to catch a cab," she said. "I suppose I'll see you tomorrow afternoon."

"Yes, er…" She was leaving as if they'd not talked for over an hour about their most passionate art interests. Never had he enjoyed a conversation with a woman so much. Krew nodded, bringing himself fully back to ground, as it was. "Yes. At the auction. Best of luck."

She wandered off, and he leaned over and twisted to catch a glimpse of her sexy wiggle. Just before she stepped out of the first-class section, she glanced over her shoulder and winked.

Caught him!

Krew sat back and…smiled.

Half an hour later, Krew slid into the limo and thanked the driver. He didn't need to give a location. That was all taken care of by Maeve. He wasn't sure where he was staying, but Maeve always choose the finest hotel in the city and something close to where he needed to ultimately be.

Drizzle coated the car windows as they pulled from the underground lot. He sat back and mused over the flight. They'd discussed da Vinci nearly the whole time. Rarely was he gifted the pleasure of talking about something he enjoyed so extensively. Art lovers abounded, but to chat more than a few minutes about any particular piece or artist was unusual.

Exhilarating.

He smiled. A sniff confirmed her perfume had permeated his suit fabric. And he didn't mind that at all.

The woman was so…in his face. Calling him *darling*. Always touching him. Yet, what did he know about women and their wiles? He'd thought he knew how to relate to a woman. Until he'd been told he could not.

His marriage to Lisa had lasted a year. They'd met in the National Gallery at a black-tie gala hosted by his father and his wife of the moment. Both had been fresh out of university and Lisa had come along with her parents; her mother the best friend of Byron's second wife. They'd quickly intuited their introduction had been a setup. It hadn't mattered. Krew had been capti- vated by Lisa's ease with speaking to anyone and everyone about anything at all. Most of the time winging it with little knowledge on the topic. She'd made him laugh. They'd dated for months. Lisa had dreams of starting a family and being a stay-at-home wife, and Krew had quickly asked her to marry him. Byron had been pleased when they'd announced their engagement. Said he'd selected well for his son.

Selected. Only now, when Krew looked back, did he realize just how calculating that selection had been. Pair him with the perfect wife, someone from old money, someone amenable to standing in the background while the husband remained a star in the spotlight. Someone who wanted to raise a family in the comfort of elegance, having her every need met.

Krew had thought he was in love with her. No, he *had* been in love with her.

Apparently, she hadn't been so in love with him. Or hadn't been able to tolerate a marriage in which she had not been emotionally satisfied. After a year she'd asked for a divorce. She needed more. A confidant. A protector. Someone who would listen and give feedback.

Rationally, he knew that was what marriage was about. Give and take. Sharing on an emotional level. If she would have said something to him, given him a chance, he would have tried.

Maybe they just hadn't been a good match. He should have known that having a wife *selected* for him could never promise him a long-lasting union. And yet, he had loved her. In his manner.

Months after the divorce, Byron had chuckled and said something like "It's your first try, son.

You'll have another shot at it." Some role model his father had been.

With a wince, Krew tossed that memory aside. Or tried to. He hadn't been able to relax and enjoy himself in a relationship since that failed marriage six years earlier. On dates he always wondered if he was saying the right thing, appropriately catering to the woman's needs. That one statement from Lisa had thrown him off course. Apparently, she had lied about being happy during their marriage.

He hated lies. It was the reason why he vigilantly sought out forgeries. No one had the right to put something out there for others to enjoy knowing it was a fake.

The limo slowed as it drove past the long line of travelers waiting in the light rain for a taxi. While he never flaunted his riches, Krew was thankful for the things money could afford him, like a driver when the weather was miserable. Out the corner of his eye, he spotted Peachy. Her hair shimmered with rain and she had no coat against the chill. Was she shivering?

"Stop the car."

The driver did so.

He told himself he was…keeping the enemy close. Not picking up a beautiful woman because it punched him in the heart to see her looking so miserable.

Krew opened the back door and called to Peachy. At the sight of him she perked up, collected her bags and slid inside the car.

"Darling, you are my angel," she announced effusively. She spattered him with raindrops while she shuffled her bags to the center of the seat. "I'm staying at the Marriott," she told the driver. "Unless…"

He tilted his head at her dramatic pause. The car started rolling again.

"Unless?" he asked.

She pushed aside a hank of wet hair from her lashes. Her lips were spotted with water droplets. He could reach over and brush them away…

"Perhaps we could share dinner again?"

"We've not determined who the winner will be yet," he said.

"Doesn't have to be a winner's dinner. I'm starving."

There was no denying he was also hungry. He'd intended to dine alone in his room, as was usual, but perhaps some company would be nice?

"My treat," she said, then directed the driver to take them to a restaurant.

"Your hotels are next to one another," the driver said in excellent English. "Someplace nearby?"

"Just take us to mine," Krew said. Then to

Peachy he offered, "I like to settle in as soon as I arrive in a new city. We'll dine in my room."

"Nice." She settled back, crossing her legs and brushing at the dampness on the skirt that clung to her skin.

She smelled of tangerines and rain. And that was about the best scent ever.

CHAPTER SIX

ONCE IN THE lobby of Krew's hotel, he directed the valet to take Peachy's bags next door and see they were delivered to her room. He took control with an ease that excited her. Of course, she knew rich men were accustomed to having their needs met, and quickly. It was something she aspired to. Someday she'd make her first million and then be able to create the life she desired. Hell, she didn't even require a million for that dream. She had a good sum in savings. A few more years at the gallery, with a pay raise, was all that she required to go country bound.

"Do you want to freshen up before we dine?" Krew asked her.

She ran her fingers through her moist hair. When wet it curled, which she rather liked. "I'm good. You don't like the rain-drenched look?"

"You're gorgeous— Er, you look great." He proffered his arm for her. "My room then."

"Lawrence!"

Peachy turned to spy two men rushing toward

them. The Daves. One held a camera, the other a microphone that was sort of gun-shaped but bigger and bulkier. Krew's sudden tight clutch on her arm directed her around behind him.

"Not now, guys," Krew said to the film crew. "The auction isn't until tomorrow. Are you filming, Dave?"

"You know we always do background shots," the man with the mic said. "We haven't been introduced. Miss Cohen?"

She was about to introduce herself, but Krew's hand at her waist stayed her. They were doing nothing untoward. And really, if he wanted to avoid *salacious* then tucking her away behind him was not helping his cause.

"Nothing to see here, Dave. David. Just helping out a fellow dealer. You know who Miss Cohen is." His hand slid into hers and he tugged her toward the lift as the doors opened.

The film crew followed.

"Tomorrow!" Krew waved them off and pulled her inside the waiting lift.

She had to catch her cane sharply against the floor to hold her balance. "They are persistent. Can't you tell them what to do? They are filming for *your* show."

The lift doors closed just before the Daves caught up with them.

"They don't need to film me walking to my

room," he announced, pressing the top-floor button more than a few times.

Peachy stepped up beside him, shoulder to shoulder. She felt a little feisty after that tête-à-tête with the Daves. With a smirk, she asked, "Is this the salacious part?"

"Apparently so."

He looked down at her, his mouth parting, perhaps to admonish her? But then his sternness softened. His green eyes seemed to invite her to a place she could live in forever. If only he'd give her permission. Because she sensed he was a guarded man. And generally, that usually meant he'd been hurt in some manner. She certainly hoped it wasn't from a tragic love affair.

When the door opened they strolled to the end of the hallway and with a tap of his keycard the door opened to a wide space.

Peachy did adore a luxurious room. And this was top-of-the-line. She wandered in, taking notice of her reflection in the foyer mirrors. Loose waves of hair thanks to the rain. And her freckles always seemed to rise to the occasion whenever the weather was a bit nippy. She looked like a movie star caught in the rain who'd been rescued by the handsome protagonist.

And yet, she cautioned herself. She'd been invited into a man's hotel room before, though it never ended with her being satisfied. But she was willing to give Krew the benefit of the doubt.

Strolling through the spacious living area to the window, she looked out over the cityscape, capped by a dash of salmon and violet above a streak of bright gold from the setting sun. The Czech capital was known as the City of a Hundred Spires, and they certainly speared the sky everywhere. It had been called the Kingdom of Bohemia centuries ago, a title that reminded of her bohemian mum. Peachy intended to tour the city tomorrow before the auction and take it all in.

She swept up her arms and tilted back her head. "Hello, Prague, you sexy city!"

A turn caught Krew staring at her, open-mouthed, hands in his trouser pockets. Oh, how she wanted to muss his tidy hair. Tug loose that tie. Generally, loosen the entire man.

"I'll have the house special sent up?" he asked.

"Perfect."

"Is this your life?" Peachy strolled before the vast floor-to-ceiling window, wineglass—and bottle—in hand. She'd set her retractable cane on the coffee table. "Luxurious hotel rooms, limos and…generally getting whatever it is you wish?"

Krew set their finished plates on the serving tray and wheeled it toward the door. A fastidious man, she suspected he liked things kept orderly. He'd hate to get a peek at her studio flat. House-cleaning was not her forte, nor an interest. If she didn't trip over it, then it didn't require tidying. Another of her mum's traits she had inherited.

"It is." He took the bottle from her, drinking from it. Drinking straight from the bottle? So he wasn't as neat about some things. "I've earned the money. No reason I shouldn't enjoy the good life it brings me."

"I don't expect you to apologize. You wear the money well." Literally. That suit must have set him back, but it was worth every single pence on his long, lean and confident form. She leaned against the frame of the open terrace door. The rain had stopped and the humidity made her skin feel dewy. "The half Windsor knot is good for travel, yes?"

He touched his tie. "It's a simpler knot. How is it you know so much about men's neckties?"

"Knot tying, of all sorts, interests me. I suspect a person can read your emotions by the various ways you knot your ties." She touched his tie but resisted the urge to tug him closer. "Moss green silk. Not quite as clear and brilliant as your eyes."

He cleared his throat and stepped back. "Does it come naturally to you, Peachy?"

"What's that?"

"The flirtation. The bold way you move around men. From the driver to the doorman to the film crew, you were working it."

"I don't work it." Did she? Well. Not when it wasn't required as a defense mechanism.

And really, a woman wielding a cane was as far from bold as it got. Since losing dance and being forced to adjust to a body that no longer embraced an easy glide through the world, she did what she could to feel good about herself. Of course, her mother had been a big influence on self-care and loving the body one was in. So instead of drowning in the sadness of being changed from what she once was, she embraced her new body and the movement it still allowed her. She may not be as agile as she once was, but her clothing and attitude could distract any man from the cane she now carried.

"This is me," she said with a shrug. "And I'm going to take your suggestion that I'm bold as a compliment. I've always embodied, well…my body. However, it's a little harder now that I've a wonky hip to deal with. I'm also very tactile. More so since my injury. I've learned to be even more aware of my body as it moves through the world. If it bothers you…?"

"Not at all. And I meant it as a compliment. I've just never… You are unique."

"I doubt that."

"Oh, you are. Like a work of art."

"Thank you."

She wasn't one to dismiss a compliment. They were given so rarely. People were just getting... meaner, less caring. But not The Brain. He may have an astute exterior, but she suspected underneath the protective shield of suit and tie the man was as exhilarating as his love for da Vinci. And his calm aura was so compelling. He could stand firmly and protect a woman, as he'd done before the Daves. And he was also able to relax and flirt, just a little.

When he again smoothed a hand over his tie she noticed something. "Darling, you're missing a button."

"What?" He looked down.

Daringly, she slid a finger along the edge of his tie and pushed it aside. Like shifting aside a door that hid his heart. He tensed. "Right there. Oh. It's gotten lodged behind your vest. Let me get it for you."

She set her wineglass on a nearby table. "May I?"

His expression said so much. *Don't touch me. Do touch me. But tender your touch carefully.*

She slipped the pearl button out from behind his vest and held it up between two fingers, dashing her tongue across her lip as she studied it. "Let me sew it back on for you." She picked up her purse and fished out the small sewing kit she always carried.

"That's not necessary. I'll have the tailor reattach it when I get home. I have more shirts packed."

"Nonsense. I'm perfectly capable of sewing on a button." She threaded the needle and returned to stand before him. "Yes?"

He eyed the needle with suspicion. "You always carry that with you?"

She nodded.

"Very well. If you must."

"Darling, I must. You can leave your shirt on since it's only the second button. But first, let's get that tie off so I don't have to struggle around it."

Peachy loosened his tie, keeping her eyes on his. She'd learned knots years ago while she'd been laid up recovering after the accident. That year of reflection and courage-gathering she had taken to studying an assortment of things that interested her online and had mastered many odd skills. Knot tying, bird calls, color mixing—which helped with identifying certain artists that were similar—even embroidery. She'd sewed all her clothing since she was about ten, but now she could embellish with embroidery. If she couldn't dance... The new hobbies had distracted her from what she had lost.

"You sure you don't need me to take the shirt off?" He unbuttoned his vest.

Peachy eyed the base of his throat where the tie had been untangled. His Adam's apple bobbed with a swallow. She imagined gliding her finger down his throat. *Yes, please, take off the shirt.* Gliding down his chest. And then the belt. And the trousers. And...

Krew held her gaze for long moments. To know his thoughts might be too much. Secrets were delicious. She winked at him, not so much flirtation as a means to let him know she wasn't going to bite. He swallowed again and looked out the window. Nervous? Or simply aware of propriety? She wished he was not but on the other hand...yes, she preferred the feeling of safety she noticed when near him.

He smelled sweet, and a little dark. Expensive aftershave, but also subtle. As calm yet inviting as his eyes. And the confidence in his stance acted as a magnet. Already her body leaned toward his as she fussed with untangling the knot.

Tie hanging freely over his shoulders, he lifted his chin to give her free rein. This scenario forced her to stand close to him. And... Peachy slid her hand carefully inside his shirt to get a good working grip, the back of her hand gliding over his chest. So warm. And his heartbeats thrummed. Hard muscle tempted her to close her eyes and melt a little.

Focus, Peachy!

Right. She pierced the button and pushed the needle through the shirt fabric, pulling the long thread out. He'd missed some stubble under his jaw. She was about to point it out but decided it may drive the man of exacting ways batty. Mmm... Touching him sent shivers through to her bones. If her skin had felt dewy before... now other parts of her were getting just as dewy.

"Not very many people know how to perform such a simple task nowadays," Krew commented. "It's nice."

"I sew all my clothes," she countered as she worked.

"You do? That dress?"

"Of course." The navy blue dress was one of her favorite patterns. Cinched at the waist and fitted around her breasts and hips, with darts in the skirt to allow it to glide with her movement. "I like my clothes to fit perfectly. You're right, sewing is becoming a lost art. Some would even say the same of housekeeping, baking and gardening."

"You do all of that?"

"Not in my tiny studio. I barely have room to stretch on the easy chair without knocking my foot on the fridge. But I have big dreams."

"As you've mentioned."

Another stab of the needle through the button and she pulled the thread out behind the shirt tab. His breathing was steady. She closed her eyes again, realizing how calm he was. Her as well. It was so rare she felt immediately comfortable with a man like this.

"I grew up in a small house with my mother. We were best friends. But as I've matured I realize that having one's mum ask to go out on double dates with you and laughingly replay some of the more illicit details of her love life to you is not what I want. I need my own place. Freedom. Peace. Yes, I have the flat to myself, but it's like living in a closet. Someday I'll marry and have a family that lives in a cozy cottage in the countryside," she spoke her dreams out loud. "Big garden, handmade clothes for the little ones. Lots of baked treats. And plenty of room to stretch out and run barefoot."

"Seems achievable. But what about the hubby?"

"Hubby?"

"Yes, your universal goal for love must include a husband? If you've plans to live out in the country will he be a farmer?"

Cheeky of him. She'd never before been attracted to a man who smelled of livestock. Or who had muck on his shoes. There was nothing at all wrong with such a noble profession but she did have her limits.

"Oh, no. He'll be as driven as myself. Probably work in the city a few days a week, then home in the evenings, where I'll have dinner and cocktails waiting. Of course, we'll have art on the walls. Fancy cars in the garage. We'll live in luxury."

"Sounds like you'll be in need of a mansion."

"A cottage can be luxurious. A simple life can be elegant and rewarding."

"A simple life with expensive cars."

"Well, I do have my quirks. An Aston Martin is also on my vision board. Go ahead, you can call me silly for my extravagant dreams."

"Sounds…actually nice."

"Doesn't it?" She tugged the thread one last time and tapped the button. "Fixed."

He brushed the hair aside from her lashes and over her ear. The unexpected touch lowered his shield a little. Peachy stepped closer. He didn't take his eyes from hers. She traced a finger up the shirt to the base of his throat…

A knock on the door was followed by the call, "Housekeeping!"

"Come in!" Krew called.

"Nice," came from the two gentlemen who entered the hotel room. The camera's light flashed a tiny green LED.

Krew swore.

And Peachy nervously gripped Krew's shirt-front.

CHAPTER SEVEN

"Guys!" Krew closed his hand around Peachy's fingers and then realized how it probably looked. Standing so close. Touching one another. He tugged her fingers away from his shirt and pushed her aside to stand in front of her. He sensed she stumbled but caught herself while he made his quick move. "What the hell?"

Dave, the cameraman, was rolling. David stepped forward with the mic. "Just doing our job, Lawrence."

"By claiming you're housekeeping? I'm going to give the producer a call. This is getting out of hand."

"If that's the way you want to play it," David said. "Keep rolling, Dave. You signed the contract, Lawrence. You know what we can and can't do while filming an episode."

Krew smoothed a hand down his chest, fully aware of his unbuttoned shirt and hanging tie. Had she touched him any longer he may have had to kiss her. Not even *may*; he would have.

He lifted his chin to eye the men. Yes, he'd signed a waiver giving up rights to reject any content the producers may wish to air. But he'd not agreed to allow his personal life on the screen.

He glanced at Peachy. "You okay?"

She nodded. Rubbed a palm up her arm. Something twanged in Krew's chest at the sight of her visibly shaken.

"I should leave." She grabbed her purse and cane but had to wait for the Daves to part and allow her to pass.

"Guys, just let her go. She didn't sign any contract with you. You have no right to film her."

Realizing Krew had a point, Dave lowered his camera and both men stepped aside. Peachy left without another word.

Krew winced. That was not the way he'd wanted this evening to go. It was supposed to be a relaxing dinner. Maybe he'd get to know his competition a little better…and kiss her? He touched his shirt. The button felt like a direct connection to Peachy. His tie still hung loose. Yet he felt sure the footage would make it appear as though she'd been undoing his tie and— Hell.

"Listen." He scuffed a hand over his hair. "Guys. Can we agree that no one wants to follow me around on this fruitless quest? When the producer suggested this hunt for the paintings would make an interesting short feature that would give the viewers a look into Byron's collection, I thought it would too. But it's turned out to be a dead end. I didn't even win the first two auctions."

"Because you're distracted," David offered. Of the two of them, the mic man was the one Krew spoke to most often. He wasn't sure if Dave even spoke when he held a camera in hand. "By that bombshell."

"Don't call her that," he said defensively.

Peachy did personify the silver screen definition of a bombshell, all curves and sensual moves, red lips and lush, bouncy hair… But the label didn't feel right for her. She was so much more than what her outsides displayed. And he'd only just begun to learn what was within her.

"I'm calling Chuck. I'm sure he'll agree this is wasted footage."

"Give it a go," Dave said as they headed for the door. "But this is season three, mate, and you really need to kick things up a bit. A little romance action is just the thing."

"Rom—" The last thing a Lawrence man ever engaged in was *romance*. "I'm not performing for you idiots."

"You don't have to. It's apparent in the way you look at her. You're whipped, mate."

With that, the two exited the room. The door, on hydraulics, slowly closed, which allowed

Krew to hear their laughter echo down the hallway. When the door finally slammed shut, he
swore and kicked the base of a chair.

"I am not whipped."

He was just being cordial to a fellow art lover.
They were both in town for the same reason.
Why couldn't he meet with her, chat, get to know
her better? Well, he didn't have to. He was perfectly fine sitting alone in his room, going over
work on the laptop.

A dull, boring evening. Had he become such
a stick in the mud?

Grabbing his tie, he slipped it from his collar.
Then he fastened the button, securing the armor
over his heart.

The following morning Peachy woke and took
a shower. The green dress with cream polka
dots and a thin lace trim had minimal wrin-
kling so she slipped it on. After scrunch-drying
her hair, she stared at her reflection before applying makeup.

Last night in Krew's room she'd taken a step
beyond dueling art dealers. She had not intended
to engage in flirtation with him. But it had been
fun. While it had lasted. Now she should focus
on the job. Heinrich would be pleased if she
managed to snag all four paintings. And, of
course, that would be accomplished.

But there was something about Krew Lawrence and his exacting ties. The desire to crack his stoic demeanor could not be ignored.

They'd shared moments last night when he'd let her see beneath his steely exterior. And she liked what she saw. She had to wonder if he even knew what his softer side was like. He'd been so upset about the film crew catching them in a perfectly innocent moment.

Well. She supposed how it was presented on the telly could change the narrative from light flirtation to something salacious. She was all in for the tease, but she'd best watch herself around Krew. She was mixing business and pleasure. It could become a royal mess if she were not careful.

Applying lipstick, she pursed her lips, then winked at her reflection. She didn't want to get Krew in trouble with his coworkers or create a scandal. He'd used the word *salacious*. Was that what he thought spending time with her would be viewed as? Was that what her past lovers had thought?

She wanted Krew to think more highly of her. To see further than other men had seen, beyond her body and curves. She was so much more! She knew art and could hold a conversation with the smartest of art dealers. She wasn't just window dressing to draw buyers into the gallery, as she'd once overheard Heinrich mutter. And she would prove that by bringing back all four paintings.

Adjusting her hair, she grabbed her scarf just as her mobile rang.

"Mum?"

"Darling, I was just thinking of you so decided to call. How it's going with the auctions?"

She briefly wondered if Heinrich had prompted her mum to check on her progress. It was possible. Her mother denied it whenever she tried to wheedle the truth from her, but Peachy had suspected for years that the two had a thing going on.

"I've won the first two and the third is this afternoon."

"Wonderful! The paintings are secure?"

"They've been sent to Heinrich's holding site. He'll take them in hand."

"Oh, dear Heinrich. I'm a bit worried about him."

Tucking her cosmetics back in the travel bag, Peachy then wandered out to find her shoes. "Yes, he has seemed to slow down a bit. Hasn't been into the gallery much. How do you know what he's been like, Mum?"

"I spoke to him last night. He sounded morose."

Yes, the man wasn't his usual bossy self of late. Grumpy with a side of arrogance. Such a joy. "I wonder if he shouldn't go to the GP and have a good onceover. He's put on some weight and he winces when he walks."

"Now, darling, you mustn't be catty."

"It's not catty to notice a man is not top of his game. Haven't you noticed?"

"I, well…" If she replied, she'd reveal whether she had seen him. "How is your hip, darling? Has it been troubling you?"

Actually, she hadn't noticed much pain at all in the last week. She'd been so focused on the auctions. And a man with a propensity for a certain calm. And charming green eyes.

"I'm fine. Just, well, you know how auctions go. They can get intense."

"Darling, you are so loyal to the gallery. Always lift your chin."

"I do. Tell Heinrich I will be successful. I've got to run. Bye."

Tying the scarf to her purse, she stroked the silk. Her mum always commented when she saw the scarf that she was such a dear to revere the gift. If Peachy won all four paintings she intended to celebrate by giving her mum something equally nice. And as for herself…

How to celebrate the win? Perhaps she'd begin looking at land listings. Really hone in on her dream and manifest by beginning the search for her future home. It was still little more than a dream, but that vision board didn't possess any power if she didn't activate it with real-world actions.

"Sounds like a plan."

Peachy headed out for the juice shop across the street. The hotel didn't offer much more than fresh-squeezed orange juice and she preferred to start the day with green juice. It kicked her system into go-get-'em gear.

Standing in the shop, waiting as they blended her juice, she perused the row of drinks lined along the counter for pickup and delivery, spying Krew's name, but misspelled as Kru. He drank green juice too? There was so much about that man to adore.

When her name was called, she pointed to his drink. "To be delivered across the street? He's my…boss. I can take it to him."

The clerk handed her Krew's drink, and winked, and she thanked him and headed out. Men always winked at her. She loved it. And she hated it. She was complex that way.

The streets and sidewalks were cobblestoned in a diamond pattern that created a work of art. With drinks in one hand and cane in her other, Peachy had to be cautious not to jab a toe into a raised cobblestone and go flying.

In the lobby of Krew's hotel, she immediately spied the film crew—if two guys could be considered a *crew*—and veered to the right before they might see her. She'd been annoyed last night when they'd barged into Krew's room, but not because of their audacity. At the sight of them Krew had literally shoved her aside. As if he couldn't bear to have her touching him. It had hurt her to be dismissed so rudely. And just at a moment when she'd felt they were starting to connect.

When the lift doors dinged and opened, she glanced over her shoulder to see one of the Daves had recognized her.

Swearing under her breath, she just caught a glimpse of the cameraman pointing his camera toward her as the heavy steel doors shut.

Rushing to Krew's door, she knocked. As he opened the door, she shoved her way in. "The Daves saw me."

"This is not wise, you coming here." He closed and locked the door behind her. "I didn't expect—"

She handed him the juice. "I was across the street and saw your name. I'm playing delivery person this morning. You like green juice?"

He sipped and nodded in satisfaction at the cool concoction. His shoulders lowered a notch. "No better way to start the day." He noticed she held the same drink. "Spinach, kale, apple, and..."

"Lemon," she continued, detailing her usual order. "With a touch of turmeric or ginger. Great minds, eh?"

Seeing his smile lessened her annoyance over last night's shove. He *had* stood before her after the dismissive move. Protecting her. Best she think of it in that manner as opposed to not wanting to be seen touching her.

Juice in hand, she wandered into his room and sat before the dining table, where his open laptop was in screensaver mode. Bright morning sunlight beamed through the open terrace doors and the scent of pastries from the same shop across the street spilled in.

"Yes, great minds," he said a little slowly. "So beyond the juice, what brings you here?" he asked. "With film crew in tow."

"I tried to avoid them. They were camped out in the lobby."

As if on cue, someone knocked on Krew's door. He cast Peachy a roll of his eyes. She shrugged and mouthed, "I'm sorry!"

"The auction isn't until two this afternoon," Krew called. "I'll see you guys later."

"Ah, come on, Lawrence. You know the producer likes us to follow your day."

"Just making some notes on the laptop. Nothing exciting going on in here."

Peachy snickered behind another sip of juice.

If only. She could think of a few exciting things to do with The Brain. One of them being to loosen that tight tie again. The man was too exacting. Rigid? No, he was more precise and organized than rigid. She'd seen the softness in his gaze when he looked at her.

"We saw Miss Cohen get in the lift."

"Is that so?" Krew called. He turned to wink at her.

Oh, yes, there was a bit of playful behind the gentleman's knotted silk.

"Listen, guys," he said to the closed door, "I'll head out for a bite to eat around noon. You can tag along to watch me try the local cuisine. Fair?"

After long moments, someone finally conceded, "Very well."

The two of them waited, listening for motion outside the door. When the distant lift dinged, Krew finally turned and sat on the sofa across from her. "You are going to cause some issues with filming."

"Me?" She crossed her legs and settled back like a content kitten. "I never cause issues. I am issue-less. Completely innocent."

Krew choked on another sip. "Not so sure about that, but I'll never argue a woman's mind. So, what brings you here so bright and early? Beyond the juice."

"Promise you won't push me around anymore?" she asked with a touch of a pout to soften her query.

"Push you— Oh. Sorry. I panicked. I didn't want them recording what was a purely innocent moment."

"It was. So you shouldn't have worried."

"I've seen the results of what me and my fellow Art Guys had thought was merely boring everyday work. Hundreds of hours of film can get edited down to minutes and in a manner that reads so different than what was originally shot."

"I suppose that is the art of creating a television show that viewers will watch."

"We were number one for months last season."

"Marvelous. I do recall that one episode with The Brawn eyeing the woman in the bikini after a deep-sea dive."

"Joss was mortified."

"Then why do you even have the show?"

Krew pressed his fingers between his brows, then splayed out his hand. "The idea of filming a short-run series was presented to us when Asher returned to the brokerage after a stint away to get his life together. At the time, it also seemed like the next step in promoting our work. Joss and I thought it might be good for Asher to have the opportunity to show his talents on camera. He was quite down on himself for a while."

"I'm so sorry."

"It was a family issue," he offered. "But all is good now. Asher's parents are doing well."

"I'm pleased. It is a lovely show. Educational, even."

"That's the part I enjoy. And the reason we continue filming. I'll leave the action and adventure to Joss and the gushing over pre-Raphaelite masters to Asher. I like to explain how things work."

"Yes, the episode where you took viewers on a tour behind the scenes in the restoration room at the Sistine Chapel was so informative."

"Fascinating, right? I admit, I also take a personal thrill in being granted admittance to such off-limits locations. It's a treat that most in our business will never be granted. We've already been slated to do an episode on Notre Dame in Paris as soon as the restoration is complete. And we're planning to do an episode on how forgeries work their way into the world through faked provenances, where I'll get the chance to interview some forgers. I'm looking forward to that one."

"Aren't the forgers behind bars?"

"Some of them. Some can elude the law with an uncanny ability. As you may know it's estimated that over twenty percent of the artworks currently in museums could be forgeries. And what museum is going to reveal that the masterpiece they've displayed for decades is actually a fake? It would destroy their reputation and hinder their ability to acquire more art. So the forgery remains on display for the world to believe otherwise. It's a weird crime."

"Not victimless."

"No, but oftentimes the ones buying the forgeries can afford the loss. I mean, well, I'm not justifying the crime. I hate forgers. Anyone who lies, really. I'm not good with dishonesty."

"That's refreshing." Peachy sipped the green juice. Truth was important. Telling a little white lie as she'd done in the pastry shop was about all she could muster. "But also telling. Have you been lied to?"

"Why do you ask that?"

"Usually the thing a person despises is what has hurt them in the past in some manner."

Krew leaned back on the sofa, stretching an arm along the dark leather. He was trying to appear relaxed but his jaw pulsed. His calm demeanor shifted so subtly. "I mean, hasn't everyone been lied to at some point in their life?"

"I hope not. Though I think my mum believes I don't know about her affair with Heinrich."

"Hammerstill?" He winced, then shook his head and laughed.

"I know. But they've known one another a

long time. It was bound to happen. Mum is a bohemian. A free spirit. Always starting new projects. Or taking new lovers. Dancing barefoot through life. Taking off on travels with nothing but a bag and curiosity. Heinrich appeals to her creative side."

"So she's on a universal quest for love?"

Peachy nodded, realizing she'd never thought of it that way. Her mother had had so many lovers over the years. Had she loved them all? Yes, in her way. Was that why Peachy felt offended at the very thought at being so free with her emotions? With love? She didn't want to stretch her love so thin. She just wanted *one* beautiful, long-lasting, forever love. Was it even possible?

"Peachy?" he prompted.

She shook her head, banishing thoughts of romance. "Are you really going to sit in here all morning when there's a little gallery down the street waiting for two hungry art dealers to come sniffing about?" she asked, desperate to change the topic.

"I had noted the gallery when arriving but thought it was closed."

She stood abruptly, gripping the cane to steady herself. "Let's go investigate!"

"And risk being filmed?"

"Doing what? Looking at art?"

He splayed out a hand. Exhaled. Then he said, "I don't know…"

Her smile dropped. She did understand he was trying to avoid a scandal. And certainly she didn't care to have any attraction she was feeling toward the man broadcast on the telly for the world to see. But she had a few hours to waste before the auction, and she did not intend to sit in her room. Alone.

Walking up to him, she stroked her fingers down his tie. "An Eldredge knot. Perfect for a morning like today. The sun is shining. The air is filled with delicious scents. Let's make an escape out the back and go look at some art." She trailed her fingers to where his tie was tucked behind his tweed vest, then back to wiggle the knot. "If you dare."

The man's mouth opened. Green eyes danced with her gaze. She sipped her juice until the scraping sound of plastic against plastic, combined with a silly crossing of her eyes, made her giggle.

With a laugh at her theatrics, he then said, "Challenge accepted."

CHAPTER EIGHT

SNEAKING OUT OF the hotel's back door felt surprisingly invigorating to Krew. With a side of stealth. To judge Peachy's bright smile, she also enjoyed the sneaking around. He was cautious not to walk too quickly, having noticed she used the cane when approaching a curb or if the pace was too brisk.

They made the gallery without sighting the Daves. Yet they were both disappointed to find it was closed for remodeling. So they continued their stroll.

"They sold modern art," Krew commented. "I wouldn't have found anything of interest anyway."

"For a client or your personal collection?"

"I don't collect canvases."

"What? I can't believe I just heard an art dealer say such a thing."

"Why would I? Art should be shared with the world. I have one wall where I hang my current passion. Right now it's a Matisse. I've had it a few months. When I've tired of looking at it, I'll donate it to a museum, then look for something else to make me smile in the mornings."

"I like that."

Peachy clutched his arm, which was about the best feeling. He liked when a beautiful woman made herself at home in his space. Even more when it was a woman with whom he enjoyed spending time. They seemed to have the same passion for specific artists—for the most part—and she really listened to him when he spoke. Refreshing.

"Let's go this way. Stay off the main streets. Out of the Daves' sight." Turning down an alleyway, he slowed to a stop and Peachy leaned against the brick wall. "Am I walking too fast for you?"

"No, I'm good. Just need to pace myself sometimes." She clutched the cane to her chest and smiled at him.

"Sorry. I'll be more cognizant of our speed."

Hair spilled over her face and before he could stop himself, Krew brushed it away. It was soft and bouncy. Fresh and free like he felt right now. When had he last engaged in subterfuge with a beautiful woman?

"You surprise me," she said.

"Why is that?" He danced his gaze over her face, taking in her lush lashes, the scatter of freckles across her nose and high on her cheeks. Her irises were warm brown but now he noticed the gold highlights circling that rich warmth.

"This isn't your manner," she explained. "The Brain always takes a limo to get around a city. And he'd never be caught dashing down the street to elude a curious film crew."

True. And yet…it had been a dare she issued. "Then I guess you don't know me very well."

Much as he never missed a weekly jog around Covent Garden, and he stayed fit working out, this silly escape was just… *Silly* wasn't the word. It was much needed. Truly, a step outside his comfort zone. Would he have done such a thing had Peachy not been along, colluding? Of course not. He'd have called for the limo and made a quick summation of the closed gallery from the back seat. On to the next gallery.

How many times had he missed an opportunity to stroll alongside a pretty woman because of his propensity to emulate his father? He never used to compare himself with Byron, but as the years passed it grew more evident their similarities could grow if he wasn't careful. Already he never seemed to stretch a relationship beyond a week or two. And that was not acceptable.

Peachy wanted a home in the country with kids and a garden? And a husband who could ensure that slow-paced yet also luxurious lifestyle? Krew had always wanted to acquire some land, but he'd never thought beyond the idea of owning a place away from the city. Moving in a wife and starting a family? Byron would cheer him on and then place bets on how long it would last. Seriously.

"I feel like I saw another museum on the drive in. Maybe that direction?" Peachy pointed down the alleyway then shrugged her fingers through her hair. So naturally undone. And effortlessly sensual. A tug at her lower lip with her teeth attracted his attention. Red lips that looked eminently kissable. "Krew?"

He realized he'd rested his hand against the brick wall, and he stood so close—their bodies were but a breath apart—but he didn't pull away. Partly to support her, but more so because…he wanted to be near her alluring Peachyness.

"Yes?"

Mouth parting, she slid her gaze down his face, taking in his tie—that she knew all the knots fascinated him—and then lower. He'd not worn the shirt with the rescued button today but he'd never part with that one now. It had been transformed by her alchemy. She had stitched her very being into it.

She clasped his forearm. An intimate move. Grounding. The bare warmth of her turned him on. The low-cut dress revealed beautiful curves.

Her neck a long line of pale marble. A sculptor's masterpiece. And when his gaze landed on her star-speckled irises, a kiss felt imminent.

The thought startled him.

Krew stepped back. Yet as he pulled his hand from the wall, and her grip loosened from his forearm, for a few seconds, their fingers glided along one another—fire and desire sparkling through his veins—and then parted.

"Right." He gave his tie a tug. "Just ahead?" He crooked out his arm for her and they strolled, side by side.

He'd almost held her hand. Krew did not care for *almost*. He liked solid, sure outcomes. Yet that *almost* had felt more exciting than actually doing so.

They wandered down the cobbled walk studying the shop fronts. This was an older part of town and the street curved around a town hall which featured an astronomical clock that mastered a main courtyard. Building fronts were brick and the diamond-patterned cobbles were well swept. The nearby river offered ferry rides but the auction began in two hours, leaving not much time to indulge in sightseeing.

Krew paused to check a text notification, while at the same time Peachy's phone pinged.

She read her text. "The auction is rescheduled?"

"Due to systems malfunction." They'd gotten the same text: Please note it will be held tomorrow at 6:00 p.m. Classic evening attire. He tucked away his phone and waited for her reaction.

And got an effusive smile.

"You're happy?"

"Evening sale! Goodie!"

"Goodie?" A visceral shiver clutched his neck. "I abhor evening sales. They're so…"

"Glamourous? Elegant? Dripping with champagne and diamonds?"

"Fussy," he decided. "You've probably not packed for it."

"I'll manage. A woman is always prepared for last-minute glamour."

"I imagine you are." Though she was glamorous all the time, whether in polka dots and heels or with her hair drenched by the rain.

"What will we do with ourselves now? I rarely get a chance to wander the city when I travel for gallery business."

Spending more time with Peachy did have its appeal. Unless of course, she thought to go off on her own. And really, what was he thinking? Getting cozy with the enemy had turned him into someone he didn't even recognize. He hadn't spent any amount of time trying to get information from her or learn her auction tricks. He had lost himself in studying her, listening to her voice, taking in her soft brown eyes and red lips as if a balm to…something he hadn't realized he'd needed. But he just knew he did.

"I understand the walk along the river is lovely," Krew commented. "How are you with longer strolls?" He looked to her cane.

"A slower pace is manageable. Though I should have worn shoes without heels."

"We'll table the riverside stroll for now. How about…?"

There were a wealth of museums in Prague. And one in particular that he felt sure she would enjoy.

"Do you want to visit the Mucha Museum?" leapt out of his mouth before he could think it through. Alphonse Maria Mucha was Prague's hometown artist.

She slid her hand into his. "You said his work was pedestrian."

The woman did not forget a single detail. He'd not begrudge her that habit. It was an excellent skill. "It is, but— Well, have you been?"

"No, and I would love to."

"Hand me your bag." He texted his driver. "I'll have the driver pick us up then bring your things back to the hotel."

"I like a man who takes control."

He tilted his head. "You do?" He could imagine so many things he'd like to control about her—but no. He didn't want to tell her what to do. Nor did he expect her to conform to his expectations. The surprise of Peachy Cohen was her appeal.

"I do." She clasped his hand and swung it gaily.

Right, then. He wasn't about to order her about, but he could direct the rest of their day. He rather enjoyed treating a woman who had no expectations of him. And he would.

CHAPTER NINE

PEACHY TOOK IN every painting, every poster and lithograph, every advertisement in the Savarin Palace, which housed the largest collection of works by the Czech artist Alphonse Mucha. She loved the curves and colors and the clean lines. Mucha was the classic starting point for many who didn't even know they liked art, and his commercial appeal had led to his paintings being used through the ages to sell everything from baby products to theater productions. The Art Nouveau style also boasted a huge hippie following. Which was probably why a love for him ran through Peachy's veins. Her hippie mother lived and breathed the man's artwork.

She sensed that Krew, despite his own feelings about the art, was even taking it in, not simply wandering past things, but rather really looking. Asking her questions. Pointing out the growth in the artist's style.

They entered the room that displayed photographs Mucha had taken of studio models for his works, and even some of his famous friends, and Krew took his time looking over the images.

"Paul Gauguin," he said of the photo taken of the artist sitting in just a suitcoat and shirt before a piano fronted by a bearskin rug. "What do you think is the story behind the missing pants?"

"I hope it's something juicy."

Peachy wandered to a display case where fantastical jewelry drawn by Mucha had been crafted in gold and precious gemstones by the legendary Parisian artist Fouquet. They'd been designed for the 1900 Paris Exposition. She particularly favored the diamond-and-emerald brooch featuring maple seed pods that looked very dragonfly-wingish.

"Brooches have sadly gone out of style," she mused. "But I still like to wear them occasionally. They are so romantic, don't you think?"

"There's romance in jewelry?" he asked.

"There's romance in everything." She wandered into the next room. "Life isn't worth living without romance."

"Not everyone is so fortunate to have romance."

"Maybe. But what a sad life." She wandered the tiled hallway where Mucha's works hung on both sides. Her heels echoed as they seemed to be the only two in the museum. She turned to look over her shoulder at him, casually following her, his hands tucked in his pockets. "I know you're sour on love, but I can't imagine a man can develop a distaste for something unless he's first had it. Yes?"

He waffled, casting his attention to the series of paintings.

"Darling, please, I can't imagine a man like you never once experiencing love."

"A man like me?" His smile was almost there. He wasn't hating this conversation.

So she continued. "Smart, rich, elegant, caring and kind."

"If you say so."

"Anyone watching the telly knows that much. I know all three of The Art Guys are single… though isn't one engaged?"

"That's Asher. He's getting married any day now. They want to do so before the little one arrives."

"They're having a baby? How wonderful! I do adore little ones. And the other? The Brawn?"

Krew shrugged. "He's got a pretty librarian who just said yes to his proposal."

"Oh, how romantic. A wedding!"

"I'll grant you that is romantic."

"I'll take it. So what about The Brain?"

"Are you asking about *my* love life?"

She gave him a shrug and tilted her head. "I'm nosey."

"You are. But… I was married for a year,"

he stated, followed by a tug at his tie. "We divorced. Amicably."

She'd not known that. It had not been mentioned on the television show. "Recently?"

"Six years ago."

"Was it a love match?"

He stepped over to her side. Looked her up and down. Assessing whether she was trustworthy to reveal some of his secrets? The best secrets involved love. Though she suspected men took the loss of it much harder than women. Perhaps because her mum was so free with her love, Peachy understood it wasn't something one should place all their hopes on. And yet, she was ever hopeful. And she knew it would come to her some day. Love could be all-encompassing and focused solely on the one. It had to be. She wouldn't want it any other way.

Finally, Krew offered, "*I* thought it was love. She didn't think so. So there you go. I've experienced love. Or what I imagine love must be. As I've said, I wouldn't recommend it."

With a moue of sadness, Peachy turned to walk in front of him as they entered a bright two-story room. The walls, ceiling and floor were covered with Mucha artworks, projected from a place she couldn't see. A bench at the center beckoned, and she walked toward it, noticing that the digitally reproduced paintings were slowly shifting, moving along the walls, and that when she held out her hand, petals from an image appeared on her skin as if fallen from a tree overhead.

How magical. Tilting back her head, she stretched out her arms. A spin would feel wonderful, but she didn't want to wobble and crash before Krew. Slowly, she curled her hand above her wrist, a flamenco move, and brought it down to one side. The movement stirred memories of dancing. Of a time when she'd felt free and whole. She wasn't sure what could return her to that feeling of utter freedom in her body now.

"How did you become so enthusiastic about love?" Krew suddenly asked. "If I can ask."

"Well, you wouldn't expect it growing up in a house where my mother was so free with her love. So many lovers. And so easily discarded. I grew to understand that too much of a good thing could spoil the magic of what I thought real romance should be. But I'll tell you my secret." A teasing smile could not be avoided. "It's because of two nuns."

Krew's brow lifted. "*Nuns* turned you on to love?"

She nodded. "After my accident, while I was recovering in hospital, a sister visited me. She was old and had the sweetest apple face. Whenever I think of her I can still feel her holding my hand. Her skin was so soft. After consoling me over my injuries she said such a terrible accident was tragic, but that I shouldn't allow it to darken my heart. That we are all here to love and be loved."

Krew managed a smirk. "A nice sentiment."

He really did fight romance with every breath! "It's only a sentiment if you make it one. You have to *absorb* love into your system. Let it in!"

"If you say so. And the second nun?"

"Ah! She was one of my physical therapists. A former nun, actually. Built like a rugby player with ruddy skin and a harsh voice. I was on the treadmill, floundering along, and some stupid commercial with lovers was showing on the telly. She noticed my disdain. With a nudge to my arm she said, 'Just love, girl. Be open to it.' And then she clapped her hands together and said, 'Now stop slacking! Pick up the pace!'"

How could a person *not* recommend love? She imagined it was the greatest feeling in the world besides dance. Despite his dismissive statement, Krew's marriage must have been terrible if it had scarred him so deeply.

And yet… Well, despite her cheerleading, for love her quest for romance continued to be fruitless.

"You think you only get one love in your lifetime?" She followed a curving line along the floor that framed the image of a spring dancer swathed in pink fabric, her hair coiling to mirror the frame. "Oh, Krew, we can have so many loves, in so many forms, it's endless!"

He paused beside the bench, hands in his trouser pockets.

"I'm in love every day," she said, turning to him. And it was true. It was the attitude that had allowed her to move on from dance and to embrace the art world. "I love my mother. I love myself. I love my tiny studio in Mayfair. Well. Mostly. It's *very* small. Confining. And I love that I found a new profession after losing dance. I love…" She turned to face him and when she wanted to tap his tie she instead drew a finger down her dress bodice, a subtle dance move. The feeling that they were the only two people in the world curled around her shoulder as if a hug. They floated in one another's orbit and nothing else existed.

"I love making new connections with interesting people who challenge me and teach me new things."

Krew's hair, face and shoulders danced with the digital flower petals. He splayed his hands. "So we're talking love in general? Not necessarily romantic? I love my life too. I have good friends, a job that I love."

"There, you see? You've not had only the one

love. Romantic or otherwise, you just have to live life to its fullest."

"Good to know. But I'll take the other option, if you don't mind. I've given up on romance. Let no nun try to convince me otherwise." He sat on the bench and patted it for her to sit beside him. She watched the digital flower petals dance across his face, knowing the same must be on hers.

"Since we're getting personal…what about you?" he asked as she settled beside him. "You must have a significant other."

"Not at the moment." Her last brief relationship had been filled with sex and late nights eating takeaway before the telly, but he'd had a job as a traveling correspondent for an independent news service so when called to his next assignment they'd made a clean parting. It had been romantic, in a manner, while it had lasted. "It makes me sad to hear you've given up on romance. But I promise, romance hasn't given up on you."

"Is that so?"

It had to be that way. For her sake. "It just may surprise you one day."

"Doubt it." He tugged at his tie.

"Exactly." She clasped the tie knot. A wriggle judged it was tightly cinched. "No romance can get beyond your shield of protection."

"Maybe it is my shield, Peach." He placed his hand over hers. Then he surprised her by stroking a finger across her cheek. "So many freckles. Like a constellation."

"I love those too," she said softly. "I have a love affair with each and every one of them."

His smile creased the corners of his eyes. "All right, I'll give the nuns a pass. You truly are open and embrace everything about life. I like that." He glanced aside and over his shoulder. "We've got the place to ourselves."

She didn't want him to stop regarding her. To take his fingers from her cheek where he traced from freckle to freckle. She didn't want to exhale because he might flutter out of her proximity like a stray flower petal.

So what *did* she want?

"I want romance," she said softly. "I want to find love. I want a home of my own where I can feel stable and peaceful. I want it all. And I know I'll have it."

"I think you'll have whatever it is you seek. You're very optimistic." His finger moved to the bridge of her nose. "These form a map of you."

That he might follow to her heart?

What was she thinking? The moment was utterly romantic, but truly, she was not so talented at recognizing truth and loyalty in men. They generally seemed to want but one thing from her. And when received? Bye, bye, on to the next.

Krew's head tilted. He studied her eyes. "What just went through your mind? I saw it."

"What did you see?"

"A shadow." He frowned. "You're safe with me, Peach."

No man had ever made such a declaration. She almost wanted to believe it. Her heart always leaped for the prize and was then tossed aside with a tattered participation ribbon. The men inevitably leaving to find someone else. Someone whole. But good riddance, because if a man had no interest in romance, he could never be true, and he wasn't the one for her.

But then why must her heart insist on such high standards? And did she need to be so cynical? Perhaps it was possible a man could be interested in her for more than what was on her surface?

When he bowed closer to her, and their noses touched, she closed her eyes. His lips touched hers gently. As if a real petal had fallen from above. Cautioning herself from grasping him and pulling him in so she could hold him, keep him, claim him for one moment of elation, she tilted her head and followed his careful, devastatingly erotic movements.

A hug of their mouths. His warm breath seared

her lower lip. Marking his place. Studying her. The scent of him filled her head with an intoxicant she could grow addicted to. His hand slid along her neck, tickling, tracing, taming her wanting skin. A firm grasp along her jaw, his thumb brushing her skin. His fingers entwined within her hair, supporting the back of her head as his kiss grew more demanding. Taking control.

And when he deepened the kiss, Peachy free-fell into a mindless plunge. Not wanting to grasp for a hold. Arms figuratively splaying wide to allow it all in. He commanded her with this kiss. No question who was in control. The man with the protective shield knotted at his throat had just plundered her defenses with a weapon no more deadly than sighs and touches.

When he pulled away, his hand sliding to caress her chin and hold her there while he studied her gaze, she tugged in her lower lip and entreated him silently. And he understood her plea.

Another kiss pulled her closer to him on the bench. He held her as he wished, and she responded with her entire body. Parts of her were climbing all over him even as she remained beside him. Anyone could walk into this room at any moment. And she was well aware that a camera could pop in to record it all.

Let them look.

Her desire went from a slow simmer to a heady want. Oh, how she wanted to slide her hands up under his shirt. Explore and take her time learning his skin and muscles. And then allow him to do the same to her. Inappropriate to grope in such a public place, though.

Suddenly Krew straightened, glanced around. He whispered on a passion-laden breath, "Not the enemy after all."

No, and that could prove dangerous tomorrow evening at the auction.

Peachy's phone pinged with a text and she ignored it. But Krew sat back, legs spread and arms resting on the bench back. "Get it."

Disappointed in their lost connection, she reluctantly tugged her phone from her purse and saw her mum had texted. She must have thought the auction was finished and wanted a report.

"It's my mum. I'll call her back."

"You sure?" he asked, getting up to wander to one of the windows.

At that moment another couple strolled into the room, gasping in delight at the digital figures moving about the walls and floor.

"Let's take a limo back to the hotel," he said, returning to her side.

Back to his room? For the usual expectations?

"Unless you want the Daves lurking outside by the tree to film our leaving?" he prompted.

She walked over to look out the window he gestured to and spied both men, who waved sheepishly at them. Maybe not the usual routine.

"Limo it is," she said, with hope.

CHAPTER TEN

At Krew's request, the driver took them on a tour of the city on the way back to their hotels. The entire roof of the vehicle was glass so Peachy leaned back and took in the buildings, loving every moment.

That was mostly due to the fact she sat in the middle of the back seat, right next to Krew, who held her hand. He hadn't kissed her again. Fair enough. She wasn't much for making out with a third person nearby. And she was still a little leery this day would end in Krew's room, him with his expectations. And her only wanting to please him and not strong enough to refuse the opportunity for intimacy.

Krew pointed out various building spires that jutted over the other rooftops. He explained that he'd only been to Prague a few times, but he liked to page through travel guides whenever he had a moment to relax. As he retained everything he read with ease, it helped for when he was visiting a new city.

"You really are The Brain." She snuggled her head against his shoulder. "How many languages do you speak?"

"Half a dozen. French is my favorite. I find it's easy to pick up the basics when immersed in a culture for a few weeks. Though generally my travels only see me in a city for a day or two for an auction or to visit an artist or client. You must travel a lot for Hammerstill."

"Not as much as you would think. The gallery is small and Heinrich's focus on the classics can generally be fulfilled through the London auctions."

"When you get your home in the country, will you still work in the city?"

"I suppose." She loved that he remembered her goal. "I'd still have to work to support myself. Maybe I'll get chickens and sell eggs?" She laughed. "Selling art was never my goal."

"Dance," he said softly. "I'm so sorry you were not able to pursue that dream. You're so graceful."

"You think? Even with this cane?"

"I've already forgotten that you need to use it. Will you tell me about the accident?"

She didn't mind sharing the struggle she had been through. While stealing something important from her, it had also reshaped her. And if he didn't notice her cane? Maybe that reshaping wasn't such a terrible thing.

"It was in New York City. Our dance troupe had won the British finals and the international competition was held in New York that year. Dance was my life starting from when I was little in those silly dance recitals with the ridiculous costumes. But, oh, did my mum love to sew the costumes! In my teens I began to focus on my skills and had a goal to go professional so I joined the troupe. We spent the first day in the US touring Times Square and tasting all the American fast foods. It was great fun. And I fell in love with Twinkies."

Krew laughed. "Those are terrible."

"They are. But oh, so soft and squishy. That's my best memory from the trip."

He took her hand and gave it a squeeze, seeming to sense she needed some fortitude.

"The bus ride to the competition was when we were hit by a semitruck," she said. "Cut the bus literally in half. I was pulled out with a jaws of life. I was taken to the ER and had emergency surgery that same evening."

He put an arm around her and pulled her against his chest. The comfort in that move stilled the tears that wanted to fall at memory of that terrible time.

"After about ten days in hospital I was able to

return to London. Had another surgery months later."

"On your hip?"

"Yes. They did a bang-up job on it, but it's not much good for dancing now. Took me a good year or two to accept that. Thank goodness my mum was such a strong supporter. She was the one who suggested I study art online while I was healing and signed me up for classes. I wouldn't have the job with Hammerstill Gallery if not for her."

"You are an incredible woman, Peach. Even after something so devastating you found a new way. Not many can do that. Those nuns certainly implanted something to make you so positive."

"Are you naturally sweet or do you have to work at it?"

He chuckled. "Ask my coworkers and they may laugh at that. Something about you brings it out of me. You seem to get me. I enjoy spending time with you and this day has been awesome."

"I get some parts of you. But you keep so much more hidden." She tapped his tie. "That's okay. I've decided I want to discover as much as you'll allow."

"I'm good with that."

"You are?"

His eyes twinkled as he looked down at her. "You don't believe me?"

Why was being with Krew so easy? And why was her romantic heart rushing forward with arms wide open? This could never be more than an affair, a few kisses that got her heart beating and her pulse racing. Because men like Krew did not have serious relationships with women like Peachy Cohen. Did they? No, they used her then tossed her aside. While never even imagining how much love she was capable of giving.

"Peach?"

She lowered her lashes and nodded. "I want to believe you."

He kissed the top of her head. "I get it. We both guard our hearts."

Yes, they did. But his confession went a long way in reassuring her that perhaps this man was different from the rest.

Krew walked Peachy up to her room. With the door open, he remained at the threshold. She swiveled her hips to face him but he noticed her misstep and lean onto the cane. The green polka-dotted dress snugged every curve of her and was cut to reveal the delicious mounds of her breasts that he…wasn't going to focus on. Not if he wanted to remain professional.

You did kiss her.

And that had been a mistake. No. Yes. Hell, he didn't know what to label it. It had happened in the moment. A good moment. So why label it as wrong? And he'd held her hand in the car on the drive here. Her body hugged against his as she revealed some deeply personal information about the accident. Another in-the-moment that he didn't regret.

She wanted to learn more about him? Why not just go with it?

With a lower of her head, and a flutter of lash, she turned and strolled inward. Krew took that as an invitation to follow her out onto the terrace where the night air was sultry and steeped with savory scents from a nearby restaurant. Much as he desired her, he didn't intend to take things any further than a conversation. That wouldn't be a wise move for a man who had just confessed to guarding his heart.

After stepping out of her shoes, Peachy leaned her elbows on the wrought iron railing and scanned the city skyline. It was a Maxfield Parrish blue, underlined by streaks of violet. "Today was lovely. Thank you."

"I noticed you limped just now. I hope I didn't take advantage of your injury with all the walking we've done."

"No, it's just my hip sometimes aches after a long day on my feet."

He wanted to brush aside the hair from her eye, which always tended to snag on her lashes, but he waited while she smoothed it away herself and recovered from the inner sadness he could see traces of in her expression.

"So the cane is because your hip aches? I thought you'd mentioned something about your proprioception?"

"It's a bit of both. The pain is from the scarring in my muscles that stretch as I walk. I can no longer hyperextend my leg, and quick movements are absolutely out. It's the inner ear thing that makes it impossible to do a quick turn or, heaven forbid, a spin. And I really have to pay attention when taking stairs or uneven surfaces like cobblestones."

Her sigh cut into Krew's heart. To have something she loved taken away from her in such a cruel manner? Devastating.

"Anyway, you've heard my sob story," she said with more vim. "And look where I am now. The top dealer at Hammerstill Gallery. Holding my own at auction against the famous Krew Lawrence."

"You do offer a challenge." More so because he couldn't keep his eyes off her. And yes, he'd also grant her some skill at bidding. "Do you enjoy working for Heinrich?"

She shrugged. "You know his reputation. No one would ever describe him as amiable. But amiable never cuts it when buying and selling valuable artworks. I do worry about his health though. He's certainly not getting any younger."

With a wince, she turned to face the cityscape.

"What is it?" He leaned on the railing beside her, shoulder to shoulder.

"I need those remaining paintings, Krew. Heinrich is depending on me. We made a deal. My commission rate will go up if I bring back all four paintings. That will go a long way toward my dream of owning a home, so I *will* strive to win them all."

Of course, he would expect nothing less. But.

"I, as well," he stated, "strive to be the best, and will win the items on my list. My dad's pride is on the line."

"Oh, darling, men tend to confuse pride with ego."

"I, well…ahem. Just know, I intend to make you another offer on those you've already won. I won't lose. I can't."

At the determination in Krew's voice, Peachy turned to face him. They stood close enough to kiss, but the tension strung between them felt like a silk tie knotted many times along the length. Each had thrown down a gauntlet of sorts. From her tally, she was winning. But she did not doubt he would go to extremes to win the next paintings. And should he make an offer for the ones she had, she would never accept.

"All's fair in love and war, eh?" he casually tossed out.

"Are we engaged in both?" she teased, finding the need to change the mood. She touched his tie. "You intrigue me, Krew."

"Both love and war are necessities to life, I suppose. I'm at my best when warring against another dealer in the auction room."

She turned to lean her elbows on the railing. The man was a challenge. He could be distracted by a wink, or a trace of her tongue along her lips, even an exaggerated sexy walk, but he was learning her, growing impermeable to her weapons. And that didn't offend her so much as make her want to strive to meet the challenge of him. How to penetrate his protective shield? And once inside, could she settle in and make herself at home? Did she want to? Why was she allowing flirtation to distract her? She should be focused on the goal. And really, she didn't want this night to end in a lackluster romp in bed that would result in him leaving her never to be seen again.

"It's getting late," he said. But he remained at the railing, his elbows propped behind him and his body turned toward hers.

"It is. We have, uh, what *do* we have here?"

He seemed to consider the suggestion for a

moment then shook his head. "You undo me, Peach. I'm running through all the things I need to accomplish before tomorrow's auction, yet at the same time trying to figure how to avoid that work and just be with you. I like spending time with you."

"Same. I also like kissing you."

"Yes, that was…better than admiring Mucha's *Slav Epic*."

Peachy arched a brow. Quite the statement, considering the *Slav Epic* was a phenomenal work. Even for a "pedestrian" artist. She wet her upper lip with her tongue and he followed that movement. "Kiss me again."

He slid closer along the railing. Touched the ends of her hair. Then trailed his finger to her shoulder and along the edge of the neckline of her dress. If he ventured lower, and closer, she might lose her careful control and grab him.

A moment later she found herself pinned against the cool brick terrace wall. He did like to press her against a surface. To keep her there in his space? To control her? She found she didn't mind when it was so gentle, even if there was always a touch of command underneath the movement.

Bowing his head, he kissed her nose, and then her mouth. His fingers glided about her waist and to her thigh. Exploring while he kissed her.

The man surprised her at every turn. Just when she thought he had assumed business mode he released his shield and took her into his powerful grasp. Destroying her will to protest. Taking in her gasps. Moaning against her ear as he hugged alongside her body. If only he would press his chest and hips to hers and then she could feel him...

Suddenly he pulled back. His mouth parted, red from their kiss, as he smirked. "I, uh, shouldn't begin what needs to end right now."

What did that mean? She wanted him back at her mouth. His hands roaming her body.

"I've got some work to do that should have been tended to earlier," he said. "Mind if we call it an evening?"

Disappointment rising, Peachy nodded. It had been a long day. And she herself knew moving beyond a kiss was the wrong move. And yet the kiss had been...everything. Had she done something wrong?

Damn it, here it was. The toss her aside part of the deal. And they'd not even had sex! And she'd thought Krew was different than the rest of the men.

"Of course." She clasped his hand. "I'll show you out."

That kiss in the museum had been an in-the-moment sort of thing. And now? Another quick taste. A tease. Or maybe just a digestif to end the night. Now, it was back to business as usual for the man.

As it should be for her.

Krew stepped across the threshold, and just when she thought he would chuckle and apologize for his silly retreat, then ask to stay, his fingers traced across hers, not quite catching a grasp, but rather seeking the touch just for the sake of it.

Her heart nudged her to ask, "You thought we were beginning something?"

He lifted his chin, his jaw tightening. Not the reaction she'd expected.

"I mean," she quickly added, "if so, it was a lovely beginning."

"Yes, it was lovely." No emotion in his tone. Not a single nuance she could read as either positive or negative. And he'd said *was*. As in it *had been*, but wasn't anymore. "Until tomorrow?"

So that was it? Move on, people, nothing to see here!

"Tomorrow then," she said.

"Good evening, Peach."

Watching him walk away, wishing for so much more, she knew that if she were to be in top form tomorrow she had best follow The Brain's tactics and keep this professional. Yet her heart ached, Krew pulling at it with every step he took away from her. He didn't want to stay and kiss her longer. Talk. Get to know her. Maybe make love. She had merely been a distraction. Nothing more.

As usual.

"May the best man win!" he called.

Peachy huffed out a disappointed sigh, then mustered, "Oh, the best woman will win!"

She closed the door and sank down against it. Since the accident, she'd had to try so hard to be noticed by men. And yet that notice was always surface and short-lived. She'd thought it was different with Krew.

Her gaze fell onto the cane. Krew hadn't seemed put off by it. He wouldn't have kissed her otherwise. Perhaps he'd just been test-driving her kiss? And he hadn't liked it enough to continue?

She swore and tilted her head against the door. "How do you do it, Mum?" Was the key to simply not care if a man waltzed in and out of her heart?

"I can't do that," she said, tears rolling down her cheeks. "I want love."

CHAPTER ELEVEN

PEACHY STOOD ON a small circular dais before a tall three-way mirror, watching as the seamstress moved around her, marking and pinning the black velvet gown. She hadn't looked forward to a morning of dress shopping. Off-the-rack items were so hard to fit correctly to her body. Which was why she sewed all her clothing.

Yet the first sight of the gown in the window had lured her inside the cozy shop that sold secondhand items. It had only been worn once, and never sat in, the owner had explained in broken English. It just needed some taking in at the waist to fit Peachy properly and the owner had directed her to an alterations shop nearby where the seamstress called her to the back room, told her it would take less than an hour for alterations and promised she would be pleased.

"You have party tonight?" the seamstress asked in her delightful Czech accent as she stepped back to study her work on the dress.

"An art auction. It's an evening-dress event."

"They sell art and dress fancy at same time?"

"That's how it's done on occasion."

The woman gave an unimpressed shrug.

Peachy stepped down, leaning on her cane, and when the woman directed her to the changing room, went inside and slipped off the dress. A discreet hand reached between the curtains and made a gimmee gesture. Peachy placed the dress on her hand.

"I love Prague," she called as she pulled on her own dress, touched up her hair, then realized as she picked up her purse that the scarf was missing.

She'd...not tied it on the strap this morning as usual. Where was it? She never forgot about it. Could she have lost it somewhere? She'd had it yesterday with Krew. Had it fallen away in the museum when she'd been distracted by his kiss? In the car?

"The city is gem," the seamstress called. The sudden mechanical cycling of a sewing machine sounded. "You find coffee and cake by wall. Sit!"

"*Dekuju.*" Peachy gave thanks using the only Czech word she'd picked up since arriving.

She found the proffered treat and poured coffee, still worried about her missing scarf. Maybe it had fallen off in Krew's room?

The coffee was blacker than midnight. But

a bite of dense lemon cake countered the bitterness with a tangy, sweet kiss. Settling on a nearby chair, she pulled out her phone, thinking to text Krew, when…she decided she would just ask him about the missing scarf when she saw him tonight. For now, it was time to learn all she could about the man she would be bidding against.

Scrolling to the Wiki page for The Art Guys, she found a link to Krew Lawrence, aka The Brain. A brief bio told her his family lived in Kensington and had owned the estate for centuries. He'd attended the University of the Arts and King's College London. Had started The Art Guys brokerage at twenty-four, which had grown to a billion-dollar success by the time he was thirty. No mention of his marriage. The featured photos were still frames from the television show. So handsome. And always in a smart suit and tie. His profile photo featured him looking directly at the camera, no smile, yet it was visible in his eyes. Shirt, vest, tie and— she couldn't discern the knot from the photo, but it must be a power knot.

Krew's moods were indicated by the manner in which he knotted his tie. She did know that much about him. His tie was his tell. It revealed his strengths as well as his weaknesses.

Sipping the coffee, and settling against a shelf

stacked with fabric rolls, she shook her head.
She didn't want him weak. *She* wanted to be
the weak one falling into his arms. Kissing him
under a real blossoming tree that rained real petals over their faces. Or held up against a wall as
he roamed kisses over her skin. She might even
be tempted to give up the next painting in exchange for another kiss from The Brain.

Pausing with the lemon cake held before her
mouth, she rewinded that last thought. Yes, so
much fun to go over. And over. And over again.
But really? She had been set on a task to bring
her boss those paintings. She would not fail. She
had to stay in the game and increase her earn-
ings so that dreamed-of home could become hers
sooner rather than later. Because her only other
skill was dance and that had been soundly ruled
out.

What woman would sacrifice so much for a
simple kiss?

But it hadn't been simple. If it had been she'd
not be expending so much thought on those
kisses now. The man lived rent free in her head
and she didn't mind that. Normally she guarded
her personal barriers. Handled men before they
handled her. Yet she'd allowed those kisses, had
wanted them to last forever. Krew could devas-
tate with a touch…

But she hadn't been designed for a man like

Krew Lawrence. She was not wealthy, elegant, nor did she run in elite social circles. She did have opportunity to rub shoulders with the wealthy because of her job. It was a skill, emulating the haughty expectations of the rich and famous, the reserved gestures and emotions. But she didn't want to put on an act for Krew, a man vehemently against lies and fakes.

Peachy closed her eyes and tilted her head against the fabric bolts. Of course she cared when a man showed interest in her. And not just any man, but one she was attracted to in return. Because she did have dreams of family. Of a real relationship that would last through the ages. Growing old with someone she loved, trusted, a real friend, would be the ultimate foil to the life she'd watched her mum lead. Not that Doris was unhappy. Her bohemian, free-range-dating lifestyle worked for her.

But Peachy wanted more. When she had children, she wanted those kids to be wrapped in the arms of both a mum and dad. To truly know they were loved. She'd never known her dad; he'd left London when Peachy was three, moving to Alaska, of all places. Mum had said he'd been drawn to the ice and snow as he was an environmental biologist. They'd never officially married, which was why Peachy had her mother's surname. Peachy had no memory of a man she sometimes crafted in her imagination as tall, burly, with dark, tousled hair he might never bother to comb because he was too busy exploring, adventuring and generally avoiding his only daughter.

Why didn't Doris have a single photo of him? Peachy had searched in the cardboard box in which printed photos were tucked away at the top of her mum's closet. Nothing. Nor was there a digital photo stored in their shared family photo cloud. And the name she'd been given hadn't led her to any answers. There were literally hundreds of thousands of Jerry Coopers in the world and dozens of them were environmental biologists. So Peachy had given up a search and settled on the fantasy ideal of an untouchable, slightly adventurous, absent father.

"Miss?"

Peachy opened her eyes to see the gown displayed proudly in the seamstress's arms.

"You try on again?" The seamstress gave the dress a shake, an impatient signal that had Peachy bounding up and onto her feet. Then she pointed to her cane. "You need all time?"

"Yes, it's for my balance."

The woman tapped her jaw in thought. Her face brightened. "You let me razzle-dazzle?"

Whatever *razzle-dazzle* implied sounded too good to resist. "I'd love that."

* * *

Krew held the scarf he'd found on the floor by a chair leg to his nose. It smelled faintly of tangerine. He inhaled deeply and crushed the fabric to his face. Soft and silken. Like her skin. Like her lips when he kissed her.

What was he doing? He'd kissed her. Twice. He couldn't bring himself to call her an enemy any longer, but what *was* she? An opponent. A fellow art dealer. An art lover. She had waxed lyrical over da Vinci's works. She'd opened his mind to Mucha's more seminal works, which he marked as a feat.

She even drank green juice to start the day. It was rare he found so many common interests with a woman. Interests that meant something to him intellectually.

She'd asked about what he'd meant by *beginning something* and he'd, typically, brushed it aside.

Why was it so difficult to tell a woman how he felt? To allow emotion into his everyday interactions? To allow himself to want? Yes, to actually want. To need. To give himself permission to seek that need. They *had* begun something. And it felt promising. Yet it also scared him.

The Lawrence men were not made for romance and love, so Krew had never had an example to learn from. Nor had he experienced romantic love—yes, even though he'd been married. What did a healthy relationship even look like?

He and Lisa were both to blame for lacking communication and not meeting the other's needs. Of course, he took most of the blame. Not there for her? It was true. Their marriage had been at a time when he'd been growing The Art Guys. He *couldn't* be there for her as much as she'd wished. And while he did not recognize that then, he did now.

He did want more. He wanted something… meaningful. He wanted to share his life with someone he cared about. Like Joss and Asher were doing right now. They were lucky to have found the person who made them happy and with whom they wanted to create a life.

Krew had a life. But it was functional and regimented and…lacking in meaning.

Just like Byron's life. The old man was probably already eyeing wife number four. Byron didn't love; he entertained, received, bought and displayed—both art and women—but never gave. He collected the paintings he crowded onto the walls in his house, but rarely really appreciated the individual quirks and aesthetics that made true art exciting.

Whereas Krew liked to look deeper. Learning Peachy's quirks and mannerisms was certainly revealing a more beautiful and unique woman every moment he spent with her.

But Byron must have loved Krew's mum? They'd been married for ten years before divorcing when Krew was six. Had they had a great romance? He realized he'd never asked his dad if he'd loved Mum. He should.

Because he wanted out of the Lawrence mold. He didn't want a wall full of unadmired artwork and a string of ex-wives. Nor did he desire a heart that never got any use. Peachy was different. And Krew liked that. He…didn't want whatever they'd begun to be just a fling.

He carefully folded the scarf and set it aside. She'd come back for it. And when she did, he'd kiss her again.

CHAPTER TWELVE

KREW ENTERED THE auction room and touched his tie. A Merovingian knot. It was unique, complicated. Solid. Tonight he would not be defeated.

When stopping into Peachy's hotel he'd been disappointed to find she had already left. He should have texted her beforehand. Why did it feel as if he'd been rejected in a manner?

A white-gloved server in black attire and white apron offered him champagne, which Krew accepted. The room, which might normally be a fluorescent-lit dull space with chairs lined in rows, had been transformed to a slightly more party-like atmosphere. The chairs were covered with black fabric. An open bar stood to the side of the room. Attendees wore elegant gowns and suits. Jewels glinted at women's necks and wrists. A flash of diamond or silver at men's cuffs. And a low melody played across staticky speakers that were not meant for any sort of formal event, that was for sure.

The Daves had been granted limited access

because of the logistics—lower lighting, alcohol and an undefined seating plan—and were occupying a corner at the back of the room.

Krew was mic'd. The producers had yet to use any of his auction audio but he'd complied with the request because he'd already pressed the Daves on this adventure. Best to offer an olive branch.

Scanning the room, he sought not the field of boring suits and colorful evening gowns but rather something— There. Hmm…no bold color today? Not a single polka dot? Was she attempting a new ploy? Something to throw him off his game? Because that dress…

The black velvet was fitted to Peachy's body as if it were a second skin. Strapless, it lunged upward to caress her breasts. He followed the curve of her side down to her waist and along her thigh where the skirt was slit so high he wondered if an incorrect move might reveal too much. But no one would call the dress lewd. It was a work of art on a figure that only Michelangelo could have sculpted.

She'd yet to notice him as she spoke to another woman who wore a hideous lime-green cocktail dress spangled with emerald gems. Krew couldn't look away. To hold her in his gaze felt as though he were claiming her. Making her his. The artist who had sculpted her had made an original that no other could copy. Should her stone effigy be placed on the block, the bidding would set world records, but ultimately, it would be best admired in a museum, where the whole world could share in its splendor.

He didn't want to share her with anyone.

Foolish man. Don't go all romantic because of a perfectly fitted gown.

Her hair bounced against her neck, loose and wavy, but even that seemed tamed, apt to remain calm and not distract a man's eye with a flyaway tendril that might get hung up on a long, lush lash. Nothing to distract from her body enveloped in black velvet.

Pity. It was just about the sexiest thing he'd ever witnessed when her hair spilled across her eye and she seemed to not notice. Why hadn't she sought to arrive here on his arm? He'd thought…

Well. Was he getting ahead of himself? Perhaps she did not feel the same as he did. As if they truly had begun something. He must have read her wrong. Never had he felt so unskilled in the art of reading a woman.

Get it together, Krew.

He set his empty champagne flute on a passing tray and grabbed another, veering for Peachy now that the lime-green concoction had sauntered off.

At the sight of him her eyes brightened. The

warm rush of adrenaline that overwhelmed his system reminded him that he did have needs. And there was nothing wrong with desiring a beautiful woman. Touching her. Holding her. Kissing her…

"Mr. Lawrence."

Her acknowledgment dropped his heart in his chest. *Mr.* Lawrence? What had happened to first-name basis?

"Miss Cohen." Krew nodded politely to her. He could certainly work the evening attire. Talk about James Bond personified. Elegant, refined, a touch of GQ model, and a whole lot of do-you-want-to-touch-this-tie? A brilliant pink silk tie.

Something tickled Peachy's nose. Then she realized the effervescent bubbles of her champagne were spitting up at her. She felt caught in a swoon. She didn't care. He was too perfect to look away from.

"You look lovely," he said. When he set his flute on the tray of a passing waiter, it wobbled and the waiter had to catch it. Krew apologized.

Something was off about him this evening. He seemed nervous.

"And you…" Her eyes dropped to his tie. "Not sure I recognize that knot."

"It's the Merovingian," he proudly stated.

"But of course, for your march into battle. Appropriate."

He tapped his lapel, then turned it aside to reveal the microphone. They were being recorded. Kind of him to alert her to that.

"I do wish you luck," she said.

"And you as well."

"Did you—" But really? Must they pretend they'd not groped and kissed and, oh, if she let her mind wander "—spend the day in your room?"

"Yes, so much paperwork to tend." He glanced over his shoulder at the Daves. A subtle hint to keep it professional.

"Of course."

"And you?"

"Shopping." She tilted out her cane to show the two wavery lines of bedazzling tape the seamstress had attached to the upper part of the metal column.

"That's marvelous."

"You think? It's called razzle-dazzle."

"I love it. Er…" He pressed his lapel. Withholding his true feelings so as not to be caught out on camera? "It is a lovely upgrade, Peach."

She tilted her head and a strand of hair fell across her lashes. Krew reached to brush it aside but stopped himself. Out of her peripheral vision she eyed the Daves. Hanging on their every word. Quickly, Krew tugged away.

"I spent some of my free time earlier considering Mucha," she said.

"Oh?"

"Yes." How her first kiss from Krew had been not her first, but the only one she would ever remember. "I love how the artist used petals to create a romantic mood."

"Yes, romance—" He frowned at her. But then something twinkled in his eyes. "I'll give you that. Mucha was a master at the romantic aesthetic. Not the time period but the…mood. I'm sure he's been responsible for spontaneous emotion and romance and…such?"

Was he attempting flirtation while under the watchful eyes of the Daves? Love it!

"Mucha's work makes me feel so alive. And sensual."

"Same— Er, I mean, how interesting, Miss Cohen. But yes, sensuality is a strong theme in that artist's work."

Peachy tugged in her lower lip behind the rim of her champagne flute. Krew's eyes arrowed onto the move. "So sensual," he murmured. And then he checked himself. "Er, yes. Uh…"

The auctioneer announced the bidding would begin in five minutes. Peachy raised her glass to him. "To love and war?"

"To…love and war."

She sipped. But he had no glass to meet her toast. Which was fitting.

Suddenly love and war did not go together in any manner for her. It had to be all for love or nothing at all.

War felt an imperfect foil to the love Krew had thought to avoid but which he now realized he wanted more desperately than anything else. Who would have thought? Yes, his life was sadly missing something Peachy seemed to embrace unabashedly. He wanted that freedom and confidence that she exuded from her every pore. And he didn't even require that desire to be drilled into him by a rugby-playing nun.

He could have it. If he allowed himself a selfless lowering of his armor. But it wouldn't be easy. Not while the Daves were recording his every move.

Peachy sat across the aisle from him. A wise choice. He appreciated that the Daves would not capture them sitting close. If seated beside her how difficult would it be to keep from taking her hand or leaning into her tangerine aura? Impossible.

Had she taken his declaration to war and love to heart? She hadn't turned to acknowledge him since taking her place and crossing her legs. To his disappointment, the high slash in the skirt was on the other side of her body—was she waiting to deploy the infamous and wildly successful leg reveal at just the right moment?

Krew tugged at his tie. The thing was too tight.

Why was he so curious about her mannerisms? Hell, was it possible he was even *more* intrigued by the notion of what he could *not* see?

Though they *had* shared some delicious innuendos. Petals and sensual art? She'd been referring to their kiss at the museum. He hoped. Certainly, the conversation couldn't be construed as anything other than a discussion of Mucha's art on the audio track. Could it?

The audience settled to a hush as waiters moved down the center aisle collecting empty flutes and handing out full ones.

The painting Krew had come for was first lot on the block so as the hammer went down to begin the auction, he focused on the small canvas as it was brought out and set on the easel. *Jar and Flower* was a work by painter Ruilin Tang from the late Ming dynasty. The ink wash style was called *shuimohua*. The small painting depicted a large black flower designed with wide, blunt brushstrokes falling from a vase half the size. The only color was a small red seal in the lower corner.

And so the bidding game against Peachy

persisted, despite his growing dislike for such moves against someone he no longer considered an opponent.

With an adjusting tug to his tie Krew glanced across the aisle...to find that the dress had fallen to reveal leg!

So this *was* war. Not love. Cursing inwardly, he forced his gaze from the woman's distracting leg.

He expected the item to go for around one hundred thousand. So he would wait until it reached eighty or so to make a bid. He enjoyed granting his opponents the false confidence of a possible win.

Peachy smoothed a hand along her shoulder, which pushed aside her hair, the movement reminding him how he'd caressed her neck while kissing her beneath the digital petals in the Mucha Museum. And then in her room, her curves had fit against his hand as if made specifically for him. If he closed his eyes he might detect tangerine—

Focus, man!

Right. He could appreciate her beauty later. When *he* paid for dinner as the winner.

With a nod, he entered the bidding. Peachy glanced over her shoulder. No smile. A lift of her chin. Determined.

Her freckles were art. Soft smatters that added

a touch of whimsy to her face. Had she enhanced them somehow so he could see them from the distance across the aisle? Big brown eyes fringed by those hair-catching lashes. Her red matte lips parted. Making him long to trace his tongue over that mouth, dipping inside her heat and dancing with her lushness. One squeeze of his hand across her derriere…

Krew's heart stuttered.

She turned to face front.

He licked his lips and…noticed the auctioneer eyeing him.

Krew nodded, making another bid. *Pay attention, man.* He had to keep his head in the game. Couldn't afford to become distracted thinking about what he'd like to do with her freckles and lips and hair and—

Another glance from the auctioneer. What was the bid at? He didn't know. Didn't care. Krew nodded.

The battle was now between him and Peachy. Enthralled by their exchange of bids, he also found it, strangely, sexually invigorating. That woman, so confident she would again defeat him, must be put in her place. But the only place he could imagine putting her was in his bed. She was so gorgeous, delicious…

Krew cursed inwardly, then nodded again. Peachy immediately raised her paddle. He nodded.

Making love to Peachy would undoubtedly satisfy like no other. But would she have him? He didn't know. She was so *much* woman.

She turned to him again, but he avoided meeting her gaze. It would be pleading. Desperate. But also erotically infused with a daring tease.

The auctioneer slammed the hammer to mark the end of the bidding. With a gesture of the hammer he announced the winner, "*Jar and Flower* goes to our visiting television star, Mr. Lawrence."

Now Krew looked to Peachy. The hair tendril fell over her eye. She bowed her head. Sucked in her lower lip. Defeated.

And he'd never in his lifetime felt so cruel.

CHAPTER THIRTEEN

"WINNER BUYS DINNER?"

Peachy hadn't noticed Krew lingering by the sales desk as she exited the auction room. She leaned heavily on her cane, seeking to calm the anxiety that made her wobbly.

Now what to do? Talking to the winner, convincing him to sell, was crucial. Yet she felt exhausted, unable to face competing with him again so soon, even if just across the dinner table. He'd proven his skill. In the art world he stood on an entirely different level from her. Way up there. With a budget she just couldn't match. She was foolish to think she could compete with him. And to even consider he'd be interested in her for more than a kiss or two…

Another step and she wobbled.

"Peach? Are you okay? You look…not stable."

"Hmm? Oh, of course I'm fine." She forced herself to smile through the pain of the loss and took his offered arm. His kindness was a balm to her scattered emotions. "You're not required to fill in the receiving forms?"

"I'll stop by in the morning to oversee the shipping, as I usually do. I'm sorry you weren't able to acquire the piece."

"No, you're not," she said softly. Heartbeat fluttering like a wounded butterfly lying on cold stone, she remembered Doris Cohen's mantra, and lifted her chin. "But love and war and all that fair stuff, I suppose."

"I suppose." He didn't look triumphant. Or even pleased. "Let me walk you out."

They walked out onto the pavement, where a car waited for Krew. He opened the back door for her to slide in. It felt as though she were stowing away with the enemy. Yet she could not fail in her mission. So she'd go along with him and see if she could convince him to sell.

Slipping off her shoes, she took some relief. Clutching the cane never helped once sitting but it served as a sort of grounding post holding her secure from flailing.

Krew gave his driver instructions to take them to a restaurant Peachy knew was the best in Prague. Ultraspendy. But he'd won fair and square so she had to be fine with allowing him to buy. Much as it cut her heart in two. And yet...now that she was in the position of loser how would she handle it? Moping and pouting was not her style.

And honestly, she wanted to see Krew triumph. He deserved that win.

"I have something for you." He dug inside his suit coat and produced her scarf. "Forgot about it earlier or I would have handed it to you before the auction."

Having it back in hand brought a tear to her eye. Peachy pressed it to her face. "Thank you. I thought I'd lost it. This was a gift from my mother and it's become a talisman of sorts. If I would have had it at the auction perhaps I would have…" She smiled sadly and shook her head. "Or perhaps it was just my time to lose. I was off my game. The best man won."

Krew loosened his tie. Remarkable. "You are my equal, Peachy. You are a knowledgeable art dealer and sharp in the auction room. A formidable opponent."

Hearing that from The Brain lifted her mood. Thankful for his kind words, she clasped his hand.

He tapped her cane. "Razzle-dazzle."

She laughed. "It's removable. Best only for glamorous events."

"Leave it. It's cool."

"You think?"

She did like the way it flashed when the light

hit it. On the other hand, did it call attention to her disability too much? "I'll consider it."

Once seated in the restaurant in the quiet back room before a wall that wavered with candle-light, Peachy exhaled a breath that she felt she'd been holding since the auction. She'd lost. But there was still the one remaining painting. And if she couldn't convince Krew to sell this one to her, perhaps when he saw she'd won three of them, he'd be more inclined to sell.

"I won't apologize," Krew started after the wine was poured.

The candlelight adorned his face, burnishing his skin and highlighting his strong jawline. She could stare into his eyes all night and never grow tired of the view. And that tie was a beacon that shouted Look All You Like! yet it defied any woman to approach too closely. She had done that. She had touched his tie, unknotted it and breached his defenses.

Pity he'd had his shield on at the auction.

"No need for apologies," she said. "It's busi-ness. I'm pleased you won."

"You're just saying that."

"No, I mean it. You've not retightened your tie. I don't know that I've ever seen you so re-laxed before. Loose. It fits you."

He beamed proudly and touched the knot.

Now there was the look of triumph she'd been waiting for.

"Shall we toast?" he asked.

She held up her glass and the scent of earth and raspberries reached her nose.

"To love, war and freckles." He pinged his glass against hers.

She touched her cheek, feeling embarrassment at the weird toast. But then warmth spread through her and she took a sip to hide what must be a rare blush.

"If I'm ever again defeated on the auction floor," he said, "it will be due to your freckles. They distract me with acute precision."

"I don't believe my freckles have ever been labeled as weapons. It's a good thing you have your shield on."

"My shield?"

"Your ties. They are your protective shield."

"I suppose. Though they weren't effective for *Melancholy* or *The Deluge*. Apparently, I've learned my enemy's ways and have overcome."

He knew so little about her. "Krew, please don't continue to label me your enemy. I don't like that."

"Sorry. You're right. The word is too harsh. But we have been rivals. Much as I'd prefer another label now." He set down his goblet and reached across the table to touch her fingers. Just the tips of them.

The unbidden touch brought up more emotion than expected. Sitting face-to-face with the man who had defeated her, and now to be touched so gently by him, and with seeming concern, tugged the muscles at the corners of her eyes. Were tears inevitable? She never usually admitted her defeat to any man. What was going on with her this evening?

"Peach?"

How she loved that he called her Peach.

"Would you excuse me a moment? Just need to freshen up a bit."

She headed for the restrooms and only when she stood in a stall with the door closed did she allow the tears to fall.

Pressing a palm to the back of the metal door, she bowed her head and sniffed. Why must she put herself through this agonizing quest for some paintings?

"Because you want the freedom and peace of owning a home," she whispered. Something different than the life her mother led. Away from the tiny flat that reminded of her room in her mother's home. Always embroiled in Doris's wild life.

But if Heinrich wasn't already aware of her value to the gallery, then gathering a handful of paintings for him now might never change that. She deserved a raise no matter the results of this quest.

And, truly, she was glad Krew had won. She didn't want to be his rival. They'd begun something with that kiss. A something that screamed for continuance.

Out by the sinks, she snatched a towel from the stack. Peachy dabbed at the corners of her eyes, then fluffed her hair. Lifting her chin, she stared down the woman who had taken on the job, filling her mother's shoes at the gallery, because at the time it was the only thing she could do after having lost dance. And she did it well. She didn't hate buying and selling art.

But she didn't love it.

And while she knew it was a waste of time to even dream about dancing again, knowing that she had settled into a career that was simply a means to make a living terrified her.

Why couldn't she be happy? Have a fabulous love affair? Get married? Create a family? Leave work behind and simply be a mother who doted on her children without needing them to be her best friends? Feel...not alone?

What would happen if she took down *her* shield? Was it truly in the way she carried herself? The way she dressed? Did she allow them to believe she was a silly woman who had no inclinations beyond fashion and makeup? Not their competition? Just a toy to use and toss aside?

That wasn't her.

Was it? It was her means to distracting from the cane, her injury, her inability to express herself as freely as dance had allowed. She liked to dress the way she did. And if men liked it too, then so be it.

But then, she did seem to attract all the wrong men.

Unless she'd attracted a new sort. Krew seemed interested in her knowledge of art. He'd even showed cognizance for her injury, ensuring he walked slowly and helping her when needed.

She tapped the bridge of her nose. He'd been distracted by her freckles. She did have a love affair with them, yet there were times even she thought they were too much. But if he liked them…

And he called her Peach.

Did she dare show him how she really felt about him? Could she trust he would treat her heart as gently as he looked after her physicality? If so, she had best stop nudging around what she wanted. It was time to separate business from the pleasure she desired. The next time he kissed her…she would not allow him to stop.

"Oh, those shoes are lovely," a woman commented as she entered the room.

Peachy lifted a foot. The black patent leather pumps had been a reward purchase after her first sale with the gallery. "Thank you. But rather uncomfortable, truth be told."

"We suffer for our triumphs," the woman declared with knowing, and veered toward a stall.

But Peachy didn't feel as though she was triumphing. And really, the only sort of triumph she aspired to might be managed by setting work aside. Just one night with the Brain?

No, you want more than that from him. And you can have it.

Tugged from her melancholy, she lifted her shoulders, gave the mirror a wink and headed back to the table where Krew stood to pull out her chair for her. The perfect gentleman.

"This looks lovely," she said of the light salad and brie she'd ordered. Her appetite had returned.

So she'd lost. She wasn't down and out just yet.

She held up her goblet to toast. "To love, war and freckles."

The man's grin could only be interpreted as an invitation.

CHAPTER FOURTEEN

KREW SENSED PEACHY had been upset. Thus the reason for her escape to the bathroom. He had won, fair and square. So why did it hurt so much to see her the loser?

Or was it an act? A means to appeal to his inexperienced heart and perhaps convince him to offer her the painting? He didn't suspect she would be so underhanded. Since getting to know her he had learned everything she said and did was genuine.

"What's your next auction?" she asked after the waiter had removed their plates and brought *becherovka*, a bitter liqueur that Krew knew the Czechs liked to consume after meals. "I assume it's *Dance*?"

"Yes. How did we ever end up with the same list?"

"I don't know." After a sip, Peachy winced. "Whew! That is…spicy, and some sort of herb I don't recognize. As for our lists, we both know they were part of a collection owned by one person."

"Yes, my father's collection. His ex-wife stole them."

Her eyes widened. "I wasn't aware they were related to you in any way when I set out to secure them."

"I know. Claudia absconded with them on the day Byron allowed her into the house to take away her things. It was a purely vindictive move on her part." He tilted the entire liqueur back in one swallow. Didn't even flinch. "I don't understand why Hammerstill wants them."

"I didn't ask." Peachy set the remains of her liqueur aside. "I've lost one of the group. I don't know how he'll take that."

"You still have a chance at the final painting."

She smiled softly, stroking the scarf she'd tied on her purse strap. "So are you headed back to London now?"

"I have a flight out in the morning. It's home for me until my secretary alerts me to the next auction. Have you heard when it is to be held?"

"I'm as in the dark as you are. Hammerstill is only learning the auction locations a day or two beforehand. He has an informant connected to the ex-wife."

"Same." Could they be one and the same? He doubted it. Lucy Ellis didn't seem the type to run in the elite art circles Hammerstill traveled. She was an online beauty influencer. On the other hand, her husband was the world's richest man, so who knew? "Would you like to share a flight home with me? I'm making a stop in Paris but I can have my receptionist book two tickets together."

"You don't have a private jet?"

Krew chuckled. "Bit flashy for me. I don't flaunt my wealth."

"I've come to learn that. Unfortunately, I already have a ticket for tomorrow afternoon. On Heinrich's tally. I really should take advantage of any generosity he slips my way."

Fair enough. Though he would enjoy another chat about art on the flight home. This couldn't be the end. "I'm glad we've had opportunity to get to know one another," he said.

Would it be forward to ask her on a date? He wanted so much more than a few stolen kisses and longing looks.

"Me as well. Even if it was as rivals."

"Rivals don't kiss," he said.

"No, they don't." She stood and moved around to sit on the chair next to him. She touched his cheek, smoothing the back of her hand against it. "You can kiss me anytime. Anywhere. Just promise you'll always mean it when you do."

"I promise."

"Is this still on?" She tapped his lapel.

"No, I tucked the mic away in a pocket when we came inside."

"Good, because... I want you to kiss me again."

He kissed her. Public displays of affection were usually absolute no-no's, so he made it quick. But just a taste of her lips was not going to satisfy tonight. "Will you come to my room with me?"

She'd heard the invitation many times before. But never had she felt so worthy, so ready, to take a chance that this time it might be different.

They kissed in the lift, and all the way into Krew's room. Always aware of her need to use the cane, he managed to direct their fumbling walk toward the terrace doors while also supporting her when their motions tilted her. Once the doors were opened to allow in the summer breeze, Peachy directed his attention back to her mouth. The man knew how to kiss. Or rather, he knew her mouth and made sure it received the exacting attention she desired. Gentle and lingering, then forceful and deep. She liked all his moves and learned that a gentle nip to his lower lip could make him growl.

His hands slid down her hips and pulled her forcefully against his body. Always he was a little demanding. Though never dangerously so. She loved it. The masculine control pushed her to the edge of cautious desire and flung her into all-out passion.

As Krew's kisses strolled down her neck she said on a gasp, "We're not dueling art dealers tonight."

"Agreed."

He lifted his gaze to hers. Emerald irises danced as if seeking her rhythm. In that moment she gauged his breaths with her own. Wanting, a little faster, needy. Dare she ask to make love? Would it happen naturally? It hadn't last night. He'd pulled away. She still couldn't be sure where she stood with the man, and it frustrated her while also drove her crazy with desire. He could not be pinned down, and that was exciting.

She wanted him. Come what may.

Tugging at the Merovingian knot, she wriggled it loose and he allowed her to pull it completely undone. Relenting his shield to her? She'd take the win.

He pushed her against the wall. Not so gently this time. His hands clasped over her wrists, pinning her there. What a thrill!

"You're the finest piece of art that I've ever put against the wall, Peach."

"Oh, lover."

Gripping his shirt, she unbuttoned it to his

vest, then kissed him hard. Deep. Unleashing her passion. And he didn't relent, following her pace with his own wanting actions. His hand pressing the wall over her shoulder caged her in.

Everything she desired was in this kiss. This man could own her if he desired. And she would surrender to his every wish. Forget romance— she just wanted this man tonight. Any way she could have him.

He kissed down to the tops of her breasts. "I want you."

"Yes," she said and followed with breathy gasps.

The dress was fitted tightly, so he'd have to unzip— He found the zipper behind her and tugged, releasing her breasts to his ministrations.

A kiss there. Oh. She sighed while raking her fingernails through his hair. He took his time, laving a searching path across her skin. Making her nipples so hard. Her heartbeats pounded. Her fingers struggled to find purchase on some piece of his clothing that might be easily torn away.

With a graceful movement, he turned her and gently laid her on the bed.

"Didn't want to spin you," he said. "You left your cane over there."

He was so considerate! Not once had he made her feel disabled or different because of her injury. He even loved the razzle-dazzle.

Now it was time for a little razzle-dazzle of their own.

As he kissed along her neck and shoulders the rough stubble of his beard tickled and teased. Everything about him was raw and wild, so unlike the calm, stoic costume he wore beneath the knotted shield. She trailed her fingers down his taut stomach and to the top of his trousers.

Yet all of a sudden, Krew pushed away from her, leaning on an elbow and crushing his fingers through his hair.

She sat up, discombobulated at the loss of his frenzied touches, his hot tongue tasting her skin, his fingers mapping her lines, angles and curves. "What is it?"

Krew swore softly and flung himself back onto the bed, arms up by his head and head shaking.

He was obviously upset. Was it something she'd said or done? Had she moved incorrectly? Why was it that he never seemed to want to move beyond kissing her?

"I don't know what I'm doing wrong, Krew."

"It's not you," he barely muttered.

That was the worst line a woman could ever hear.

"It's…" Again he swore. "You're so different, Peach."

The second-worst line, surely.

Peachy tugged in her bottom lip with her teeth. She slid alongside him, gliding her hand over his bare chest. The muscles were solid; the protective shield extended. A shield she thought she had permeated. He panted. It was difficult to come down from such a hot and heavy make-out session. And she didn't want to. But something was bothering him.

"Are you sure I didn't do something wrong?"

"Never," he said.

"I thought we'd agreed we are no longer enemies." She glided her finger down to his trousers where she'd been so close to unzipping him. The man was certainly ready to go. But how to rev up his engine again? "Talk to me."

He exhaled heavily. Sat up onto his elbows. "I like you, Peach. But this feels so different."

"You've said that. I'm sorry, but you do know that different doesn't sound very appealing."

"Huh? Oh. No! Different is good. Amazing. You're perfect. And I just feel like…"

The man whom the world knew as The Brain—rich, famous and one of the most talented art dealers she'd ever crossed paths with—had just called her perfect. That didn't track.

"Don't say that. It's just little old me, Krew. There's nothing perfect about me. I can't even walk without a cane. Why are you threatened by that?"

"The cane doesn't bother me. It's part of you. And it's a little sexy, actually. It adds a touch of vulnerability to your strong and sensual persona. Peach, I'm not threatened. It's just…" He sat up and stroked her shoulder, tangling his fingertips in the ends of her hair. "You want real, romantic, passionate love. I…don't know if I can give you that."

Clutching her loose dress against her breasts, she kissed him before he could say more. She moved to straddle him and he fell back to lie on the bed again. She stroked his hair. Tapped that cute little mole above his eyebrow. His eyes, so liquid and green, pleaded with her.

"Let's take this slowly, shall we? Romance isn't even tops on my vision board. Right now? I just want to have sex with you. I don't want your crazy-good kisses to stop tasting my skin. I want your hands all over me. I want…"

He tilted a look at her. "No romance tonight?" His sweet expression held her heart. This man was one in a million.

"I don't think I could concentrate on anything else but how you make me feel."

"Same. I want you, Peach."

And despite her wanting to plead that it mustn't be only one night, Peachy stuffed away that unrelenting desire and kissed him.

And Krew spun her to lay on the bed, tear-ing her dress lower and making sure any stray thoughts about romance were quickly side-tracked to the real and exquisite now of making love.

CHAPTER FIFTEEN

KREW ROLLED OVER in bed beside the most beautiful woman in the world. Once he'd gotten beyond the worry that she was only looking for romance and roses, and could focus on enjoying her body, the two of them had really synced. In proof, he had sent Peachy into delicious convulsions of ecstasy. He'd had a few orgasms of his own.

Making love to her had guided him beyond her surface and into a deep understanding of how she worked.

And he wanted more. All of her. All the time.

He was moving ahead too quickly though. Last night had been the result of their flirtatious few days together. Did she want more from him? Could he give her more? He knew she wanted romance. And he, well…

He checked his watch. Not even 7:00 a.m. He had some time before his appointment to sign off on the *Jar and Flower*. And then it was off to Paris. A side trip Maeve had scheduled so he could stop into a client's home and oversee the delivery of a sculpture. The client, ever in need of coddling regarding where and how to place the art they purchased, eagerly awaited Krew's direction.

He nudged his lover gently and kissed the curve of her shoulder, noticing more freckles there. "Peach?"

"Morning," she muttered drowsily. "I was lying here with my eyes closed absorbing the heat from your nummy body. So delicious."

She sat up and he tickled his fingers up her back. More freckles here and there. She had them everywhere.

"Is your flight to Paris this morning?"

"It is. First, I need to stop by the auction house to supervise the packing of *Jar and Flower*. Still, that gives me at least another hour."

"Well then. Let's find a way to spend an hour."

"I have a few ideas. Shall we…do something salacious?"

Peachy would have liked to cancel her flight and fly with Krew to Paris for a day but her ticket home was already paid for. Now she was left to wonder at what came next. Had last night been a fling? The culmination of their flirtations? Would he, soon enough, decide he'd had a taste of her and wasn't satisfied? She shouldn't be so hard on herself, but her dating history made it impossible not to consider.

Best to not get too attached and just be thankful for the time she did get to spend with Krew. Once again, she was settling for what she felt others wanted and not grabbing what she desired.

Now she had the tough task of letting Heinrich know she'd failed. Back in her room, she picked up her phone and scrolled to Heinrich's private number. He answered after one ring.

"I'm sorry," she said, "I wasn't able to acquire the *Jar and Flower* ink wash."

A heavy exhale rumbled over the connection. She knew that growlish sigh. He was angry.

"Who got it?" he asked.

"Mr. Lawrence. The Art Guys—"

Hammerstill's outburst of swear words surprised her. The old man did have a tendency to punctuate his conversations with oaths, but it was usually *bloody this* and *bloody that*, not the extreme words he let fly now.

After a fit of coughs that made her wonder if he needed water, he hissed out, "He is the last man on this earth who should have that painting." *Cough, cough.* "You must get it from him." *Cough.*

"I tried. I can make another offer if you'll let me know how high I can go. What is the urgency

in getting these specific paintings? I don't understand."

"Because I told you—" *Cough.* "Your damn
mum! Why do I continue to do so much for Doris
after all the trouble she has caused me? Where's
my…?" She heard something scatter in the background and crash. He must have knocked things
off a counter. "Winded," he said.

Yes, and he didn't sound good at all. "You
need to lie down, Heinrich. I didn't mean to
upset you. I'll talk to Mr. Lawrence about purchasing the *Jar and Flower*."

"Have to…hang up. Get that painting!"

The line went dead.

Peachy stared at her phone. What on earth?
The man had sounded one step away from complete heart failure. And so angry. And why had
he mentioned her mum? What trouble had Doris
caused Heinrich that was related to the paintings?

She knew her mum had originally sold the
paintings. She'd been working at the gallery right
around the time of Peachy's trip to New York
with the dance troupe. But what did that matter? What was going on with these paintings that
Heinrich had a conniption over the loss of one?

Scrolling to her mum's contact, Peachy waited
for her to pick up. No answer.

She left her a message. "Mum, there's something we need to talk about."

* * *

The Daves merely waved as they met Krew at the doors to the auction house. Yes, folks, the behind-the-scenes stuff was never interesting. Overseeing the packaging of an artwork? Why even bother sending the crew?

But they were merely doing as expected. So he intended to be quick about it. Then they could hop on the flight to Paris with him. His client there was always thrilled to be filmed and hammed it up with hopes to appear on-screen.

Probably a good idea Peachy hadn't come along. Give her a rest away from the camera. He wouldn't see her for two days. It would be a challenge. When he'd vacillated over a tie this morning, he'd gone with the pink one. Because it held a subtle tangerine odor. Wearing her scent against his skin was the next best thing to being close to her.

Krew had asked to look over the *Jar and Flower* before it was packed for shipping to the London office. It was laid out for him on a table in the packing room.

He'd already started The Art Guys when Byron had acquired this from Hammerstill, and he'd only glanced at the painting a few times when it had hung in the living room at his parents' estate. It was small and had been tucked beside the mantel where a massive Ming vase had partially blocked the view of the piece if one were standing at a certain angle from it.

He leaned over the table to reacquaint himself with the work. *Shuimohua* painting was not his forte. The canvas was generally paper or silk. The actual painting was more about the emotion than a precise depiction of a particular object. Only black ink was used. The vase was created with one quick line; a downstroke, then a twist to the right, and then upward to form the rectangular receptacle. The flower was formed by a thick brush; a dab and pull there, there, and there for the petals. The intricately drawn name along the lower right corner was accompanied by the trademark red seal Tang put on most of his works, but not all of them. Krew had viewed a few of his works over the years and the brilliant crimson seal was almost a work of art in itself.

Then he saw it. Something about the seal...

He nudged the edge of his littlest fingernail next to the curved corner of the seal. It was... raised. It should not be. The ink should have permeated the paper. Especially on a centuries-old work... The paper did still have noticeable tooth to its texture. So he tested his fingernail along another corner of the seal. It wasn't removable; it had been printed onto the paper. And yet...

The smell of ink was oddly prevalent. And the red had altered slightly, showing more of an orange tinge to it. Almost as if the crimson had faded.

Snapping his fingers with irritation, Krew gestured toward the clerk. "Hand me that loupe."

A small viewing magnifier was placed in his hand. Krew leaned over the painting, eyeing the details of the tiny seal. But he didn't need the loupe; the differences in brushstrokes and paint tones were obvious. This seal was almost a deep orange. And it showed evidence of fading, which was never apparent in Tang's other works. So obvious he should have recognized it when it was on the bid floor. Why had he not—

That tendril of hair falling across her lashes. Her red matte lips parting. Desire had overwhelmed him, challenging his ability to focus.

Krew swore under his breath. Once again she'd distracted him. Yet why? Could she have known the painting was a forgery? No, she'd wanted it as much as he had. He should have examined it before auction. But this painting had been in the previous owner's care for eight years.

Byron Lawrence had owned a forgery? Had he *known* it was a forgery? Was that the reason he now wanted it back? It was worth absolutely nothing.

No, his father couldn't know. Byron had never had the skill to judge a fake from the real thing.

Krew had once stopped him from purchasing a Renoir for that very reason.

"Where's the provenance?" Krew snapped, not caring that it sounded rude.

"Here, sir."

Krew took the packet and sorted through the papers. A digital scan of an invoice, gallery consignment report, a few photographs. It had once been part of a rotating collection of the artist. It listed a half dozen museums worldwide it had toured. Until one of the museums had offered it on the block to raise funds for new construction. That dated to about eight years ago. It listed Hammerstill Gallery as the seller to Byron Lawrence. As for *where* Hammerstill had acquired the work before the museum auction there was no other listing. A period of about a decade was not accounted for.

Was Hammerstill selling forgeries? There was a possibility Heinrich had not known. Much as the gruff old man with a penchant for seeing The Art Guys fall had become a stick in their craw, Krew honestly believed he wouldn't purposely sell something he knew was a fake. It wouldn't look good for his gallery.

He and Peachy were on the hunt for four specific paintings. So perhaps it was just the one that was forged. Made the most sense. It would be incredible were all four were fakes.

Leaning over the painting, he fisted his hands either side of the work.

Behind him Dave asked, "Can you narrate your concerns, Lawrence?"

Right. He'd forgotten he was being filmed.

And yet, what might be the implications if he revealed the fake? Would it smear the auction house? Trace it back to Byron? And ultimately…him.

He touched his tie. The lavalier mic was on. Actually, this…was an opportunity.

"Is there a problem, Mr. Lawrence?"

A new voice. Karlson Richard, the owner of the auction house, offered his hand to shake and Krew did so. In the next few moments Krew worked the angles in his head. He could reveal that the painting was a fake, possibly embarrassing the auction house on camera if they did not know. If Mr. Richard did know, then he would be implicated in a crime that neither of them would want to be involved in.

If he didn't say a thing, and walked away with the painting…

Truth was, he couldn't just declare it a fake without sending it to the lab for a forensics examination. He had a man in London whom he employed for that. It could take weeks once he had the painting in hand. So until then, he wanted to keep this close to the vest.

Out the corner of his eye, Krew sighted the camera crew. Diligently filming.

Mr. Richard waited for his reply.

"Uh, just checking all the paperwork."

"You know we assure that everything is in order."

But had they encountered a forgery before? In the years Krew had been in the art world, he'd never experienced a bad deal with the Arthouse. And Richard was the utmost professional.

"Send this one directly to my office," he instructed the manager.

"Not to the usual holding house?"

"No, I want it sent to the London office."

"Of course, Mr. Lawrence. Will you be overseeing the packaging?"

"No. But do give me a few more minutes with it alone. The crew will want to get some shots." He gestured to the Daves. Krew tucked the paperwork under an arm, and again shook Mr. Richard's hand before he strolled out.

Now he muttered to the mic, "Guys? I think we've got something here."

David, manning the shotgun mic, lifted his head and zoomed over to Krew's side, followed by the cameraman. "What is it?"

"That segment we planned to do on forgeries?" Krew nodded to the painting. "I believe we can start right now."

CHAPTER SIXTEEN

THE PARIS STOP took the entire afternoon and into the evening so Krew's client invited him to stay for dinner, which he did. He'd also invited the Daves, much to their thrill. They rarely got to participate in the rewards of what the camera recorded. Many times he and his colleagues stopped for a bite to eat at a street vendor or attend a cocktail party hosted by a collector and he'd notice the Daves' hungry looks. Well, for once he was glad for the meal and the shared camaraderie.

Now that they'd arrived at Heathrow airport, Krew sighed as he waited for the pilot to announce that passengers could deplane. One more painting left to obtain for his father. Or really, three. He had to get those other two from Peachy. Why was he doing this? To help the old man avenge his pride? As Peachy had said, men had a manner of confusing pride and ego. And truly, it was all ego for Byron Lawrence.

Just as it had been a matter of ego for him

back in the Prague auction house. He'd walked out with a possibly forged artwork. He hadn't wanted to implicate the auction house or make any accusations until he had proof, but the move didn't sit well with him now. Ego. Pride. Yes, they were two very different things but also easily confused. Pride would have seen him walking away from the forgery, reporting it to the police.

Had he slipped up? No. The forensic examination would prove him correct, and only then could he feasibly look toward reporting it as a crime.

And he was growing more inclined, day by day, to let Peachy have the remaining painting. She wanted to advance at the gallery and earn more income so she could create a little country life for herself, something a woman who had lost one dream through a terrible accident really deserved. A place to feel at home. At peace.

Krew could grant her that wish with a slash of his black credit card. The expense would barely matter to him. Buy her some land, build her that cottage. Add in some chickens and…the family. But that was ego thinking. It would polish his ego to know he'd helped her in that way. Pride would see him standing hand in hand with her, giving her help if she asked, and if not, cheering her on.

It was a monumental realization.

He did hope Peachy could have the family she desired. And something nudged at him that maybe he could be included in that dream. Was he getting romantic again? She tended to bring that up in him.

And he didn't mind that at all.

Following his fellow passengers out of the plane, he called Peachy as he strolled through the jetway. She didn't answer so he texted.

Back in London. Can I stop by and pick you up for an evening at my place?

By the time he reached the curb for pickup she'd answered.

See you in a few hours. The Kelvin knot is appropriate for an adventurous evening inside.

Smiling and telling the driver to take him to Mayfair, he tugged loose his tie and began the Kelvin knot.

As Krew's limo pulled up outside Peachy's place, a cheery red-polka-dot dress was the first thing he noticed and his smile was irrepressible. Peachy slid into the back seat and kissed him. Soundly.

"I missed you…" It had only been a day, but

yes, he did. He intended to tell her about the forgery but it could wait until he had solid forensic proof. The driver began their route home.

"I missed you as well." She snuggled up and hugged him. "So how was Paris?"

"I don't know. Took the limo to the client's home in the sixth, and then headed straight back to the airport."

"Pity. I understand the d'Orsay is exhibiting Degas for a few months."

"I do know that. I'll jet over one night to sit and enjoy it when I don't have to worry about the Daves following me around."

"You act like you merely tolerate them, but they're your friends really."

"Yes, I suppose. Whenever they're up for pints, I rarely refuse. And we did have a nice dinner with the client."

Later, after a round of lovemaking that had begun the moment he'd closed his penthouse door behind them, they sat in the kitchen sipping wine. Peachy sat on the counter before him, wearing nothing but his shirt. The one she'd sewn the button on. She smelled like tangerines, sex and wine. Sitting before her on a chair, he pressed the side of his face along her bare leg and closed his eyes.

"Best. Place. Ever."

Peachy stroked her fingers through his hair.
Always making contact.

He liked it. Hell, he craved it. She made him
see the world in a new way. She allowed him to
see himself in a new way. Maybe romance could
be a thing for him. He did not have to be destined
to become a womanizer like Byron. Because he
couldn't imagine brushing aside someone like
Peachy Cohen as just another pretty face to keep
on his arm and then discard when he tired of her.

"Have the Daves ever followed you home?"
she asked.

"Not allowed to." He kissed her thigh then
stood and fit himself between her legs as he nuzzled into the warm nook between her hair and
neck. "Does it bother you? Them following me?"

"I don't want to be a television star," she said,
"so I hope they'll edit out anything with me before putting it out for the world to see."

"No hunger for fame?" He straightened and
she stroked a fingernail down his bare abs to
the top of his boxers. Mmm… "What about
your dancing? Did you not aspire for shows,
the stage?"

She set her wineglass aside. "I had an aspira-
tion to dance on that television show that cou-
ples dancers with stars. And then there was the
summer I intended to study in Spain. But now…
it's just easier to leave that dream in the past."

He kissed her neck. Her wanting moan fueled his growing desire. Yet it was countered by his genuine concern for her. He'd never cherished a person in his life. No, not even Lisa. Not properly, anyway. But he did now.

Her cane was hooked on the end of the counter. He liked that she'd left the razzle-dazzle on it. "So now the dream is having a country cottage with kids and goats?"

"I never mentioned goats."

"I know. But aren't they cute? A guy could have a goat or two."

"Could a guy?"

"Yes."

"I don't think they'd like living in this penthouse, and I wouldn't rule out a country property." He sensed he'd just jumped too far ahead in the narrative. Is that what romance did to a guy's head? He'd take it. "So tell me about Spain. You studied there for dance?"

"I was supposed to go there the summer following the accident."

"Oh."

"The flamenco style of dance is a passion of mine." She stretched up one long arm, her wrist twisting in what he knew was a flamenco move. "Or it was." Her shoulders slumped and she teased at the band of his boxers. "I had paid for a year of study with a private school. I never did get a refund because I was so embroiled in my injuries and healing for that summer that it didn't even occur to me to ask for one."

"Is that where the polka dots come from?"

She smiled curiously. "You think?"

"Well, the style of your dresses, so fitted and with a flirtatious ruffle here and there, have a touch of the flamenco to them."

"You're right, my clothing is inspired by the dance. I'd actually made myself a *bata de cola*, the traditional flamenco style of dress, and had hoped to take it to Spain with me. You're so smart, Krew." She hugged him. "Do you like the tango?" she asked suddenly.

"I've never danced. But I do enjoy watching others dance the tango. It's very…"

"Push and pull," she provided. "Love and hate. Like us."

He was convinced that strand of hair was designed to fall over her lashes specifically to tease him. Krew brushed it aside, then traced the galaxy of freckles from one of her cheeks, across her nose and to the other.

"We're not so extreme, are we?" he asked. "I don't believe I could ever hate anyone."

"What of love? When love strikes, it's not because you allowed it."

"You think so?"

"I know so." She wrapped her legs around his hips and he hugged her closer.

This felt intimate and right. But could it ever be love? Despite what Peachy believed, Krew knew that love hurt. But there was nothing at all wrong with enjoying the company of a beautiful woman whose touch made him relax and feel comfortable in his own skin for the first time in a very long time.

He brushed the hair from her forehead. "You make me forget about everything but the present. I need that. I need…you." He surprised himself with that statement. "I mean, yes, I feel like now that you've been in my life these past few days, it's as though my entire body is exhaling, relaxing. Taking you in. I like you, Peach."

"It is nice between us. I feel safe with you."

"You've not felt safe with others?"

She shrugged. "I've never been physically harmed by a man, but sometimes they can be so callous. Especially about my injury and the cane."

"I like the razzle-dazzle." He kissed her forehead and then her mouth. "We've done salacious—now how about we try…untoward?"

CHAPTER SEVENTEEN

THEY'D WOKEN TO watch the sun rise. And while Krew was in the shower, Peachy reclined on the big leather sofa sipping the juice he'd blended for them. Extra ginger provided a tangy bite. Wrapped in but a blanket from his bed, she had no desire to dress. But he had to head into the office soon, so she should consider it.

Her attention strayed to the Matisse on the three-story-high brick wall before her. It was a small painting depicting a French country scene. Such a marvel that the man had the discipline to own but one painting. And then to donate it to a museum when he tired of it. More collectors should do the same, she decided. Art truly was something that should not be owned but rather shared with the world.

She had only prints in her tiny flat. Spending money on art wasn't in her budget with the dream of home ownership in her future. But she'd get there.

Krew breezed out, bringing his subtle, darkly

sweet scent along with him. He settled onto the sofa, nuzzled into her neck—oh, did she love it when he kissed her there. It sent the best kind of tingles throughout her body. Her toes curled under the blanket.

"I hate to leave so quickly," he whispered. "My car is already waiting," he said after the kiss. "You take your time here. The door automatically locks when you leave."

"Are you sure? I can grab my things so you don't have to worry about leaving the place to me."

"I don't mind. Do you?"

"No." She glanced to the Matisse. "But I may have to spend a little time with her before leaving."

"Take all the time you want. I like to sit and stare at her as well." He kissed her quickly. "I'll text you when the viewing is finished…?"

"Yes."

He grabbed his stainless steel travel mug and headed for the door.

Peachy leaned back, her bare legs jutting out from the blanket. She lifted a leg and pointed a graceful toe. He whistled. And she laughed, not realizing it had been a sexy move, but apparently it had been.

"Bye, lover!"

He'd left her alone in his home. Half-naked

and nestled in his blanket. In the presence of a gorgeous Matisse that truly did demand long and relaxed observation. What dream had she been dropped into?

What had begun as a rivalry had taken a sharp turn to the right. And that right felt so good. Dare she believe that love might have found her? Only a nun could tell her for sure.

Her phone, left on the coffee table last night, rang. With a smile from the thought about the nuns still tracing her mouth, she picked it up. "What is it, Mum?"

"Oh, darling, I just heard your message."

"That was sent a day ago, Mum."

"My phone has been weird lately. Losing the charge. No matter. How did the auction go?"

"Mum." Who cared about the auction? That she had lost! There was something more pressing to discuss. "Why is it Heinrich is so hell-bent on recovering these paintings? And why is Heinrich so enraged about something *you've* done that he calls trouble? What is it you are not telling me? What's going on?"

A heavy sigh was so out of Doris's range. Peachy shifted on the sofa to lean on the thick arm. Soft morning light streamed into the room, highlighting the bookshelf in a corner that she intended to snoop through later. "Mum? What is it?"

"I suppose I must give you the details."

"Details? What is going on? I suddenly feel as though you and Heinrich are plotting something."

"Perhaps a bit."

Peachy's jaw dropped open and she stood, clutching the falling blanket against her bare breasts. She wandered back toward the bedroom as her mum spoke.

"Did I ever tell you about Richard Francis?"

Peachy shook her head, not following this sudden conversation detour. "Who?"

"The man I was dating when you were a teenager. Right around the time you joined the dance troupe. Remember Dickie?"

Oh, him! How could she forget? Her mum's lover for three or four years. The hippie who had sported a long, uncombed beard, linen kaftans, with a penchant for spending hours secluded in their shed while he painted his next "great opus," as he'd so often put it. As a teenager she'd never been compelled to get to know him, converse with him. Too busy with the dance troupe and chasing her dreams.

"I remember those awful striped kaftans. And he always wore sandals," she recalled. "What does he have to do with me getting these paintings?"

"Everything, darling. Everything."

That sounded so ominous Peachy felt her equilibrium tug. She aimed for the unmade bed and landed on it just as a wave of dizziness overtook. Whatever her mum was about to say, perhaps prone was the best position to be in to hear it.

"It was right about the time of your accident, darling. I was struggling at the gallery. Hadn't made a sale in months."

"Oh, Mum…"

"Now listen, I panicked. And I needed to make some quick cash, so I went to Dickie and he was very willing to help. He did adore me so."

Peachy stopped herself from rolling her eyes. It was Doris's manner to believe most men who walked the earth should adore her. And…who knew, perhaps they all did.

"At the time one of our clients had a wish list of sorts," her mum continued. "Works that he wanted me to keep my eyes peeled for. It was long, but I thought to help him with a few if possible."

"Mr. Lawrence?" Peachy asked, dreading the answer. The only obvious guess since she knew her list was specifically paintings Krew's dad had once owned.

"Yes, Byron. Handsome man. Old money. Entitled. He was always giving me the eye and asking me out for cocktails."

Had Krew's dad dated her mum? The horror! "Did you…date him?"

"Oh, darling, no. He was not my type. Too stodgy."

Krew thought he was like his dad. Obviously not. There wasn't a bit of stodge in Krew. Yet, her mum did have a thing for Hammerstill. And Peachy would label Heinrich as stodgy as they came.

"Anyway, I showed Dickie the list, and… Well, he was able to help me."

"How? I'm not following you at all, Mum."

"Darling, Dickie was a professional forger."

Peachy rolled to her stomach on the bed and clutched the loose sheets. She didn't have words.

"That's why you were never allowed in the shed, darling. He was a marvel with a paint-brush. Taught me so much about light and which brush to use for the desired effect. He managed to whip up a few things on the list rather quickly."

"Whip up…?" Images formed of a hippie in a linen caftan slapping paint across a canvas. And yet, if he'd produced something on Byron Lawrence's list…it would require such skill.

"You know Heinrich never paid much mind when I brought in new works to be sold. He trusted me so long as the provenance was ship-shape. Well. He adored me. Always has, always

will. I could do as I pleased. And doctoring provenances is a sort of talent of mine, I suppose."

Even more shocked, Peachy could but gape
and shake her head. She didn't want to hear this!

And she did.

"Dickie created three of the works on the list.
I, in turn, sold them to Byron Lawrence over a
period of about a year. Safer that way to stretch
it out. Didn't want it to look suspicious."

Suspicious? Peachy gripped a pillow. She almost dropped the phone. Her body shivered.
It felt as though her mum had just physically
punched her.

"Darling? Peachy, you can't blame me. I did
what I had to do. No one was the wiser. But now
that they've come back on the market, Heinrich
insists we get them back in hand."

"He *knew* they were forgeries?"

"Not at the time of sale. I eventually told him
one night while we were...ahem."

Peachy closed her eyes tight at that *ahem*.
Her mum had never thought it embarrassing to
share occasional sexual details with her over the
years. But anything involving her boss was best
blocked for fear of lifelong trauma.

"He was upset with me, but not for long,"
Doris continued. "We'd thought we'd never hear
another thing on it. That the paintings would
hang in the Lawrence estate forever and either

the gallery would close or we'd die before they ever went on the block again."

"Mum, you sold forgeries to Krew's dad. Krew Lawrence. A world-famous art broker who has a show on the telly!"

"You think I would purposely put out those works knowing I might get caught? I had to do it, darling. All those medical bills— Oh. Oh, dear. I swore I would never tell you that."

"The medical bills?" That could only mean *her* medical bills. Her mum had never mentioned a financial hardship at the time of her accident. "Mum?"

"Well, yes, Peach dear. The National Health Service covered your final surgery after returning to London. But the bills incurred while you were in America…"

At the time, she'd asked about the bills that had tallied up in New York and her mum had brushed it aside. *Don't worry about it, darling.* And so, she had not. All her focus had gone into recovery. She'd been determined to walk normally, to even regain the ability to dance. Unfortunately the inner ear injury had other designs on her future.

"We just didn't have enough," Doris finally said. "And I've told you I wasn't selling much at the time."

So paying a medical bill would have been

an incredible hardship. And Peachy knew the medical system in the US charged exorbitant amounts. "Mum, why didn't you tell me?"

"It had to be done. Peachy, don't get maudlin now that I've told you. I didn't want to give you another worry, more stress when you needed to be strong to heal."

"Oh, my god."

"And now we're making it right," Doris said with a lilt.

Her mother had committed a crime? To cover her medical expenses. And Dickie… "Where is he? Richard. Dickie. Whatever his name was."

"Oh, darling, he passed a few years ago. Cancer. Nasty stuff."

Peachy crossed her legs, sitting on the center of the bed, feeling so far away from the delicious lovemaking she and Krew had shared in this space just hours earlier. Life had punched her again. And this time she had no clue how to lift her chin and deal with this one.

"Those paintings mustn't fall in anyone else's hands," her mum insisted. "We need all three returned. Then Heinrich and I intend to burn them. End of story."

"Burn them? Three? But…there are four paintings on the list, Mum."

"Yes, well." Doris sighed. "One of them *is* an original: I needed some means to bring in a larger sum beyond the commissions I made on the others. I want you to find it. To bring it back. To place it where it belongs."

Which was where? And which one was original?

This was so much to take in. Peachy felt as if she'd stepped into a new timeline. Another world. Her mum and Dickie and Heinrich were all involved in something so impossible. Yet horribly real.

Which meant Krew may have just won a forged work of art—if it had been one of the three, which, doing the math, was likely. The Brain was known for sleuthing out forgeries. How had he not known before bidding on it? *Had* he known? No. Couldn't have. There had been no public viewing beforehand and she had spent most of the preceding day with him so knew he'd not privately visited the auction house.

A thought struck her. "Is Claudia involved as well?"

"Oh, no, darling. She just happens to be a friend of mine. She's rather crafty, yes? Getting revenge on her ex like this. I'd admire her if it wasn't such a travesty for Heinrich."

"If she's your friend why didn't you offer to buy them from her before they went to the block?"

"Heinrich did. She wasn't having it. Seems

she wants to revel in watching her ex lose out on all the paintings. She knows his dealer is after them and is being as elusive as possible. But I also believe she wants him to bid on them. Just to see him have to buy them all over again. Brilliant, actually."

"Mum, that's awful. The woman is awful. What you and Dickie have done is…" So awful!

"Yes, yes, but I did it for you, my dearest one."

Peachy swore inwardly. Putting the blame on her? That was incomprehensible.

"You don't want the gallery to be embroiled in such a scandal," Doris said. "Heinrich's heart couldn't handle it."

Peachy recalled the man's erratic breathing and coughing when she'd spoken to him.

"I think you should check on him," she said. "He didn't sound well when I spoke to him yesterday. And…" She caught her forehead in hand. "I've got to absorb this information. I'm at…"

She stopped herself. There was no reason to tell her mum she was at Krew's home. It wasn't necessary. And really, she didn't want to share the best thing in her life with her mum right now. Because it felt as though if she did, her mum would find a way to ruin that.

If she hadn't already done so.

"Goodbye, Mum."

She clicked off even as Doris was speaking.

Tossing her phone onto the bed, Peachy caught her head in her hands and yelled into her palms.

She felt as though she might crumble if she moved the wrong way. No cane could provide support to the upset she'd just received. Her world had just been shoved, and she wasn't sure how to balance anymore.

She needed some advice. But the only one she trusted was also the man who had more than a few times proclaimed them enemies.

Enemies who set aside their business rivalry and had allowed their hearts to intrude. So much for her hopes for romance. This information would spoil any future they may have had.

She touched her lips, recalling Krew's gentle touch. A touch that had grown masterful and knowing with every moment. Had she ever had a man trust her so completely that he'd allowed her into his shielded heart?

No, never.

If she told him about this forgery mess he'd never look at her the same again. She had lost him. And she'd only begun to realize she may have caught him.

On the way back to the office, Krew took a call from Chuck, the producer. He was excited about this discovery of a forgery and wanted to film every move Krew made around it. It would be days before the painting arrived in London but the forensics scientist had already made time on his schedule and agreed to allow the Daves to film his process.

Chuck was less willing to budge in other areas. Krew had asked him to leave Peachy out of the segments, saying she wasn't necessary to the forgery angle. Chuck refused.

"Why would a dealer from Hammerstill Gallery want to obtain a forgery?" Chuck asked.

"I don't believe she knows it is a forgery."

"Or maybe she does and she'd hiding something. I've seen the preliminary footage. That woman is a bombshell. We need her."

"I feel as though you're trying to leverage her to achieve something that's not true. I'm very willing to expose myself for having bought a fake, but I will not allow you to use Miss Cohen to increase ratings."

"Just stay in your lane, Lawrence. We need to investigate all angles of this. She may be innocent, as you've said. And if so, she'll come out smelling like roses in the edits. But if not…"

Krew blew out a breath and shook his head. Before he could reply, Chuck said "Cheers!" and hung up.

And Krew swore as he tucked away his phone. The last person he wanted to get hurt by this discovery was the only woman he cared about.

Yes, he cared about her.

But could he if she *did* know something about the forgery?

After arriving in her loft and unpacking her things, Peachy's mind was fixated on the news her mum had just laid on her. A crime had been committed—many crimes, in fact—because Doris had needed to cover Peachy's medical bills. The feeling that it was all her fault was immense.

Would Krew pull up his knotted shield should he learn the truth behind the paintings? Of course he would. He was just and upright and would never tolerate such a crime.

Her phone pinged with a text notification from her mum. Not willing to call and talk to her directly?

With a huff, she opened the message app.

Claudia has released Dance to this auction house in Andalusia. Auction tomorrow. You must reclaim.

"Andalusia? Bloody…" It was the absolute last place in the world she wanted to visit, even if only for a day.

Peachy tossed her phone aside. Because of her mum's foolishness she was now forcing Heinrich to buy paintings he couldn't even resell. That *she* couldn't resell. The paintings would have to be destroyed. There went her hopes to make big commissions. To gain a raise. To start looking for a home of her own. She'd already spent close to half a million on the first two. So much more than she imagined her hospital bills could have ever tallied.

Doris should be the one attending these auctions, trying to retrieve her crimes and tuck them away.

On the other hand, Peachy did owe her. At a time in her life when she could barely support the two of them, Doris had done what she had to to make it work. Peachy couldn't fault her that. But if she'd told Peachy about it at the time they could have taken out loans, made it work. Legally.

She texted back: Is this one a forgery?

No answer. If *Dance* wasn't the forged painting, then why bother to retrieve it? So it must be. Peachy punched the air in frustration.

She turned to face the wall where she had pinned photos and pictures that made up her vision board. A stone country cottage laced in climbing roses sat at the center. Surrounding it were images of grassy fields, hedgerows, children laughing, some delicious vegetables piled in a basket. A few of her favorite works of art.

And there, right beside the country cottage, was the photo of The Brain.

She tapped the picture. Inspiration. And admiration. She'd been trying to manifest her future life. A home to call her own. A place where she could be happy, peaceful, fulfilled.

A tilt of her head took in Krew's brilliant green eyes. Had she somehow…?

"Did I manifest *you* instead?"

A thrilling shiver traced her neck and cheeks. But only for a moment. Because even if she had manifested the best thing currently in her life, it couldn't last.

She hadn't heard from Krew all day. He must be busy…learning the painting he'd just won was a fake?

She had to tell him. He'd never forgive her if she did not. But if she did, could he forgive her her mother's crimes?

Either way, it wasn't going to be good for her.

CHAPTER EIGHTEEN

THE FOLLOWING MORNING Krew called Peachy.

"Sorry, I've been so busy," he said. "The next auction is in Andalusia."

"I know. My, uh, er... Heinrich's contact came through with the info."

"As did mine. I've booked a flight for us this afternoon. I'll send a car to pick you up. I have more filming today as we receive the *Jar and Flower*, so I'll see you in a short bit. And kiss you then."

He'd taken care of everything. The perfect gentleman.

"That's sounds perfect. I'll see you later. Thank you, Krew."

They hung up and Peachy went to her closet to pack. She would tell him... Hell, when, *how* could she tell him? If he were filming the receiving of the painting today then he would surely discover its secret. Unless it wasn't the forged piece. According to her mum, one of the four on her list was apparently an original.

She hoped the painting Krew had won was the original. She needed all the delay she could get before she had to rip out her heart and toss it to the ground before him. Because he wouldn't respect her after he learned the truth. And for as much as he admired her differences, this new truth about her very different life certainly couldn't overcome the crimes that had been committed.

Krew took Peachy's hand as the plane began its descent toward the Seville airport. She'd been quiet most of the flight. Extremely out of character for her.

"Are you okay?"

A heavy sigh preceded a nod.

"You're not," he concluded, which he'd discerned from the absence of a smile. "Tell me what's bothering you? Is it your hip?"

"No, it's fine. It's… Andalusia."

"The city? What about it?"

She turned to face him. The sun shining through the window highlighted the freckles sprinkling her nose. "Remember I told you I had signed on to spend a year studying dance in Spain? It was here in Andalusia. And I thought I'd be okay with coming here, but I'm feeling out of sorts. Thinking about what I lost and what I'll never have again."

"Peach, you should have said something earlier." He traced his thumb along her jaw and cupped her cheek gently.

"Wouldn't have made a difference. I need to attend this auction."

"I'll be at your side, holding your hand. Promise."

"That means a lot to me. But I feel as though if I see a flamenco dancer I might burst out in tears."

"Nothing wrong with that. Tears are okay."

"Are they? I can't imagine you've ever cried."

"We men don't do that sort of thing," he joked.

"But it's okay for us weak women?"

"Wow, you really are feeling down on yourself. Come here." He pulled her close and gave her a hug just as the plane's wheels touched the tarmac.

Peachy buried her face against Krew's neck and inhaled, losing herself in him instead of in the anxiety that threatened to overwhelm. It worked for about thirty seconds. When the flight attendant announced they would soon deplane she recalled the other anxiety-inducing information that she needed to tell him.

It had to happen soon.

Krew checked his watch. "We'll go straight to the auction house as we only have an hour before it starts. I booked us a room and can have the driver deliver our things there. You going to be okay?"

She smoothed out her dress skirt and nodded. "Are you sure you want to spend the night with me in a hotel? What if I win this one?"

He kissed her. "Then you buy dinner."

They arrived at the auction house with about twenty minutes to spare. Peachy had touched up her makeup in the car and as they got out, Krew handed her the cane, still razzle-dazzled. Out of the corner of his eye, he saw that the Daves, who had also just arrived, were going through their gear half a block down. He acknowledged them with a nod but Peachy didn't notice as she fussed with the scarf tied to her purse and then gripped both hands on the head of her cane.

"You seem out of sorts, love," he said. "Is it still being in the city that's unnerving you?" They had driven right by the school that she'd been slated to attend. He'd held her hand and had felt her heartache deeply.

She shook her head. "Seeing the school was difficult, but I'm stronger than I realized. It's just… I can't keep this inside any longer. I should have told you during the flight but it was so nice just to sit there and hold your hand."

"Peach?" He smoothed a hand up her back and finally she met his gaze. He'd kiss her but he couldn't be sure the Daves wouldn't capture that on film. Well, he knew they would.

"There's something you need to know about the *Jar and Flower*. All of the paintings on our lists. Or actually, three of them."

But that could only mean… She knew? Krew's heart dropped.

He started to speak but she put up her hand. "Please, just listen. I spoke to my mum yesterday. Oh. Your tie is crooked."

She adjusted his tie. And…he allowed it because her touch was always welcome. This small intimacy felt like his very breath to him. Yet, it cut him to the bone anticipating what she was about to say.

"Mum told me something devastating. I have to tell you. I won't keep secrets from you. *Jar and Flower* is, or rather could be, a fake," she said. "Hammerstill wasn't aware until— Well, it was years after my mum had sold the paintings to your father that she finally revealed the forgery scheme to Heinrich. So he's not to blame either."

"A forgery *scheme*?" Sounded so much bigger than one single painting.

"I swear to you, Krew, I had no clue."

"I studied the ink wash the morning after the auction and determined much the same."

"You— It *is* one of the fakes? But why didn't you tell me?"

"I—" Yes, why not? Because part of him had suspected her? Or because he'd hoped she wasn't involved and it could all be brushed aside, leaving their relationship untarnished? He so wanted this to be real.

"I didn't want to say anything to anyone until my suspicion was confirmed," he said. "It's currently at the lab undergoing a forensic analysis. But now, you've just gone ahead and outright confirmed it."

The Daves were filming and getting much closer now. Krew took Peachy by the arm and turned her away from the camera. He'd not yet turned on the microphone he wore on his lapel, thank goodness.

She gripped his forearms. "You have to believe I had no clue. It's a— Oh, Krew, it's a twisted and tangled thing. One of my mother's old lovers forged the paintings so she could…"

He wasn't sure he wanted to hear more.

But he needed to hear it all.

"Could what? Profit off my family?"

"No, that's not— Well. Yes, it could be viewed in that manner. Mum needed money to pay my medical bills. Her lover offered to fake some of the items on your dad's wish list."

The confession was insanity. The Daves had drawn closer. He should tell them to back away, but Krew's instincts switched toward getting this information on film. It was all linked to the forged artwork. He subtly turned his mic on.

"There's more than one fake?" he asked, needing her to confirm it on record.

"There are three." Her lip wobbled.

His heart did a dive. "Who was the painter?" he asked her.

"His name was Dickie. Richard something or other. I knew him vaguely. At the time I was young and hadn't much interest in conversing with any of my mother's lovers. Mum said he died a few years ago. But Krew, it makes sense to me now why Heinrich insisted we get all these paintings back in hand. He wants to destroy them so they are taken out of circulation."

"He didn't seem so concerned about the forgeries when my dad bought them."

"I told you, he didn't know! My mother didn't tell him."

"How could she have slipped a forgery by Hammerstill?"

"Well, you don't know my mother. She's very…not so much manipulative as…beguiling?"

Krew gave her a gobsmacked stare. Seriously? Of course she would soften it to make it sound as if her mother were merely some sort of misguided honeypot. *She's a honeypot… Too bad she's broken.* Cruel words spoken by that dealer at the first auction.

Had the daughter the same inclinations as her

mother? Could he believe Peachy had nothing whatsoever to do with this crime?

"Heinrich has always had a crush on my mum," she continued. "When she was with the gallery she had free rein of the place. And…apparently, she had a talent at faking provenances."

Krew winced. He did not want to hear this even though he needed to hear this. How could Peachy get involved in anything so…illegal!

"So it's your mother who should be prosecuted for the crime."

"No! Krew, don't you see? If we destroy the paintings it all goes away."

"Save the cash my dad laid out for forgeries. Four of them, Peachy."

"No, mum said there were only three. Which makes no sense because there are four on my list."

"Is *Dance* a fake?"

"I don't know. Mum didn't specify which one was the original of the four."

"Peachy, I just spent one hundred and twenty thousand euros on the Tang. I know it's a fake because the seal was poorly reproduced."

"We'll buy it from you. I'm sure Heinrich will insist."

"Buy it? This is a crime, Peachy. I've already begun recording details about the painting for the—"

"The show? You're going to implicate my mum? Me?"

"No, I…"

Peachy clutched his forearm. "I just wanted you to know the truth. I thought I could trust you to keep it between us." When she looked to the side, she gaped. Having sighted the camera crew, she shook her head. "That can't go on record. It's not necessary to tell the world if it's a problem we can easily solve. Your dad will be compensated. And it's not as though she did it for malicious reasons. Mum did it to pay my medical bills. Our insurance didn't cover the stay and surgery in New York."

Krew wasn't sure how to process this information. Her mother had been knowingly involved in a crime to help her daughter. A daughter who apparently had no idea what had been going on behind the scenes.

"I need to think about this," he finally said.

Peachy stepped back. "I want to always be truthful with you. We've…" She glanced to the Daves. "Well. I had thought we'd become… close."

They had. And he wanted that. More than anything. But now that hopeful future had been intruded upon by something that he could not fathom. A massive lie that had involved not only him but also his dad.

Slipping his hand inside his suit coat, he pulled out the lavalier mic and shoved it in his pocket. Without a glance to Dave, who he knew was having a conniption, Krew leaned in and whispered to Peachy, "You are a complication."

And as he drew away from her sweet tangerine aura he winced. Wanting to kiss her. He made a silent promise to them both that he wasn't walking away, that he just needed some time to process it all.

"We should get inside."

"I don't know if I can."

"You have to. We'll figure this out."

"Okay. I'll be right in. I need to…check my makeup."

Peachy stood at the curb, head down. She shrugged one palm up her opposite arm then kicked at her cane.

Krew's heart was torn. And that was a feeling he'd sworn to never again experience. Damn romance.

As the Daves followed him in, Krew kept turning to where Peachy stood at the curb. She lifted her chin, hearing her mother's words. *Darling, lift your chin. A good fake can get by with so much.*

How telling that statement was now. Never in

her life could she have imagined what it would eventually mean.

You are a complication. How it hurt for him to label her that way. But it was true.

Involving Krew further in the mess her mother had created was the last thing she desired. But she'd had to tell him. She wanted Krew untouched by the wickedness of it all. Too late. Had she thought secrets delicious? Ugh! This one was awful and heart-wrenching. If she could reverse time and go back and ensure he hadn't won *Jar and Flower*, she would. The man had never asked to be involved in scandal. He was good and just and the best thing that had ever happened to her.

And her mum had messed that up beyond repair. There was nothing she could do to convince him otherwise. And really, now he had excellent fodder for his show. At her expense. He'd not said he'd protect her. Stand by her. Be there for her.

She wanted him to pull her into his embrace. To kiss her. To reignite the passion that had seen them through nights with barely an hour of sleep.

But she'd lost him with the truth. Perhaps it was for the best. He was too good for someone like her.

Krew had chosen his side. And it was not hers.

CHAPTER NINETEEN

PEACHY FELT NONE of her usual confidence as she walked down the aisle between folding chairs, relying heavily on her cane for support. Instead of her usually fun polka dots and ruffles, she'd worn a plain emerald dress today, still fitted, but the only detail was cream buttons at each of the cap sleeves. She hadn't wanted to dress in anything that reminded her of what she'd lost. Once in Andalusia, she'd thought to experience heartbreak all over again by being in the city she'd never gotten to visit. A city that might have been her home while she had honed her skills and furthered her dance study.

Yet the real heartbreak was even more devastating. Here she'd lost the trust of her lover. The only man she cared for. They had begun something. And now it would end.

She found an aisle seat and crossed her legs. Touched the scarf on her purse. Looked over her shoulder. She didn't see anyone's face or if they noticed her because her thoughts raced.

She clutched her cane. While not experiencing a dizzy spell, she felt out of balance with the world.

"Is that seat beside you taken, sir?"

At the male voice she looked across the aisle to find a dapper gentleman with a smart tie waiting for a reply from an elder gentleman sitting one seat in. The older man removed his auction catalog from the folding chair and nodded that Krew could sit.

Peachy glanced down the row to her right. All seats empty. He could have sat next to her. Instead the enemy had seated himself in the most opportune position to go to battle.

Her heart dropped to her gut. But she was cognizant to lift her chin. She smiled at him.

He nodded once. Then adjusted his tie and took in the room. She hadn't noted what type of knot formed his shield today. She was really off her game. Now all eyes were on them. Whispers she couldn't quite make out and glances back and forth between her and Krew made her more nervous. What did they know? The film footage hadn't been aired, and no one could know of their relationship. Had Krew already alerted someone to the crime she was desperately trying to cover up?

She twisted at her waist and spied the Daves at the back of the room. Dave nodded to her. Gave her a thumbs-up. Krew had mentioned they'd begun filming for a show about forgeries. The Brain could bring in big ratings for the show by revealing the forgery to the world. While also implicating her. How could he possibly keep her out of it?

Pressing a hand over her erratic heartbeats, Peachy turned to face front and uncrossed her legs. She felt undone. Out of sorts. Not at her strongest. This was not happening. She was trapped. By the one man she had thought to trust. A man who had promised to stand at her side and hold her hand.

From the corner of her eye, she saw the cameraman move as close to the barrier as possible and adjust his lens. Zooming in on her?

On stage the auctioneer announced they would begin. The hammer landed on the wood auction block and the first lot was brought out to display.

There were a dozen items before the final *Dance* painting, but the bidding went swiftly. Forty-five minutes later, as the audience, now dwindled by half, waited for the final item to be placed on the block, Krew glanced at Peachy. She couldn't read his expression, though if she were telepathic she could likely sense him asking her to surrender. To give up. Make it easy on herself.

"Ladies and gentleman," the auctioneer said,

"we've had to pull the *Dance* because of an un-expected issue. The auction is now concluded. Thank you all for attending and your gener-ous bids." With one final tap of the hammer he brought the sale to a close.

Peachy mouthed to Krew, "Did you do that?"

He shrugged. "It wasn't me."

CHAPTER TWENTY

KREW HAD NOT attended an auction where a lot was pulled moments before it was scheduled to go on the block. Sure, there were occasions where an item may be crossed out of a catalog because for various reasons it was no longer available. What had happened that they'd pulled *Dance*? Had it been confirmed as a forgery as well?

Peachy had said that there were three forgeries. But she had four paintings on her list. How could he know which of them was the real thing if he'd not held *Melancholy* and *The Deluge* in hand and examined them?

Now that the auction floor had cleared of the dealers, the film crew made its way past the barrier and stood but four feet from Krew. Peachy had swiftly exited. All he wanted to do was rush after her. Because he cared about her. And he wouldn't put up a shield or pretend otherwise. If they whispered about The Brain having an illicit affair, then so be it. Because it wasn't illicit to him. To him it was a joyful thing. And he was all in for protecting Peachy.

And yet, he'd come here today to win. And he was determined not to allow the Hammerstill Gallery to get away with selling forgeries. One of Heinrich's dealers had purposefully introduced forgeries onto the sales floor.

On the other hand, while he felt the mother should pay for her crimes, if the paintings could be gotten and kept out of the public's hands—destroyed—it would cause no one harm. And there was the fact that the real criminal, the forger, was dead.

Krew gestured to the Daves as he strolled down the sales floor. "We're done here. Why don't I buy you lunch across the street. Meet there in twenty minutes?"

Both men exchanged looks. "Miss Cohen hasn't left. We're staying."

Ahead, he spied Peachy in a plain green dress. No polka dots. It hadn't occurred to him during the flight how uncharacteristic her attire was. She was on the phone talking with someone and seemed agitated.

"She hasn't granted us permission for use of her image on the show," he said calmly to the men.

"You can handle that for us."

"That's not in my job description."

With that dismissal, the Daves conceded and left the sales floor.

Krew turned but had lost sight of Peachy.

"I'm here at hospital now," Doris Cohen said over the phone. "The ambulance picked Heinrich up a few hours ago. Oh, darling, I'm so worried for him."

Peachy's mom had just explained how Heinrich Hammerstill had been found in the back of his gallery sprawled on the floor. He'd suffered a heart attack. Her mum was frantic. She was never good at handling trauma. Whenever Peachy had skinned a knee or cut herself as a child, she'd been left to do triage while her poor mother had to lie down on the sofa because the sight of blood gave her nausea.

"Do you want me to return to London?" Peachy asked. She glanced over her shoulder, spotting Krew talking to the Daves.

"Would you, darling? Oh. I really need you."

"Of course, Mum. I'll hop the next flight. I should be there after supper."

"Did you get the *Dance*?"

"Uh, no. It was pulled from the auction. Do you know why they would have done that? Is Claudia behind this?"

"I have no idea. It's not even… Well, it's an original."

"This one is the original? But then why have me go after it?"

"I feared if you knew that you would drop the quest to retrieve it. It's *my* original, darling. Please, Peachy, you must get it."

"Your original. You mean, *you* painted it?" The story behind her quest just got crazier and crazier. And yet, there was no denying her mother was a painter. She'd been painting for all of Peachy's life, her swirly abstract style one that Peachy knew she would recognize instantly. "You didn't copy another work?" She hadn't seen the painting but the auction catalog had described it as an abstract Spanish dancer.

"No, darling, it's my own work. I promise."

"But they've pulled it. I don't have a clue why or where it's being held." And with Heinrich in the hospital the crazy just increased. "Do you want me to come to London or not?"

"I do. Maybe you can have your Mr. Lawrence nab it for us?"

Of all the audacity! "Mr. Lawrence will not be involved in anything remotely criminal, Mum. Now I'm hanging up. I'll…see you later."

Peachy tucked away her phone with a huff. What a bloody mess! And while she wanted to run to Krew for support, a hug, a solution to this problem, she knew she couldn't ask that of him.

She spied Krew still talking with the camera crew. The conversation they needed to have could not be done in public. And…she wasn't prepared for a private one either. She had to get home to London. She'd figure out what to do then.

"Mr. Lawrence!"

At the prompt from the auction manager Krew paused in his pursuit of Peachy. He'd asked to speak to the manager but this was terrible timing. Would Peachy leave without saying goodbye? Or course, he'd not handled her revealing the truth behind the forgeries well at all, even if she did have every right to expect animosity from him given what she'd told him.

"I have a few moments," the manager said and nodded that Krew should join him. "I understand you have questions about *Dance*."

Down a short hallway they turned to enter a room where the lots were held before going on the block. They now awaited packaging and shipping instructions from the winners.

The manager stopped before a painting that featured a dancer. Or the idea of a dancer. It was modern and the entire work was circular, a sweep of paint strokes emulating a figure in a violet-and-pink swirl. He'd noticed it a few times when visiting Byron. Loved the colors, and the allusion to a flamenco dance.

"*Dance*," the manager said. "Artist unknown. I've been unable to match it to any current artist's style."

"Why was it pulled?" Krew leaned in closely to inspect the canvas. It wasn't ugly nor was it masterful. The movement in it was delicious though. Truly a dance.

"The seller called. She's, well, she's…"

"Claudia Lawrence," Krew said. "Or rather, she's taken her maiden name again. Claudia Milton."

"You know her?"

"She's my dad's ex-wife."

"I see. Apparently, she wasn't happy with the venue. That was the only reason she gave. Quite unacceptable. But we do strive to keep our clientele happy."

"Are you aware that the former Mrs. Lawrence stole this painting from her husband, along with three others, and is selling them in order to get back at him in some vicious manner?"

"I never involve myself in the personal minutiae behind the sale."

Krew gave the man a dressing-down. "Well, you should. So far my father has not gotten the police involved, but should he…" He let that loose threat hang for a moment. No one wanted to get involved in criminal or legal action. "How much did Miss Milton want for the work?"

"A hundred thousand. But it's no longer for sale."

Hardly worth that amount. Maybe twenty or thirty thousand at best. The woman truly was greedy.

"Everything is for sale."

Krew stood back and gave the painting a long perusal. Amid the swirls he could make out the faint white dots that must be part of the dress. A graceful hand swept above the head. And then it struck him. The figure was…familiar.

"Are you making an offer under the table?" the manager asked. "The provenance states it was created less than a decade ago. And there are no other known works by the nameless artist. Why is this work so important to you?"

"My father was devastated by the loss of these much-loved works of art. I did try to make this go smoothly, away from leering media, by snagging the painting at auction, but…"

It was a gentle but meaningful threat.

"A hundred fifty thousand," the manager said. "I'm sure the seller would be very pleased with that. And I'll have *Dance* wrapped and shipped directly to your London office."

That was highway robbery. And he suspected Claudia would not see any more than sixty percent of that price.

Peachy's mum had been trying to pay off her daughter's medical bills?

Krew cursed inwardly. He tugged at his tie knot. A circular Aperture knot. He'd thought it fun, relaxed, something Peachy would like. She hadn't even commented on it.

He should have gone with the warrior-like Merovingian.

He held out his hand and the two men shook. "Deal. But I'll take it with me today."

CHAPTER TWENTY-ONE

PEACHY ARRIVED AT the Royal London Hospital and was directed to Heinrich's room. As she walked through the hallways a shiver enveloped her. Last time she'd been here she'd been a patient. A fond recollection of the nun with the apple face and soft hands lifted her chin. *Just love*.

She'd thought to touch love, but it had been fleeting.

She found her mum sitting beside Heinrich, holding his hand. The hand-holding thing shouldn't be weird. Doris was consoling the man. And yet, the vibe Peachy got was more than friends. Not unexpected, but—everything in her life just weirded her out lately!

She set her purse on the end of the bed and leaned down to hug her mum. She smelled of the rose soap she crafted and sold at flea markets and her soft linen dress had been misbuttoned up the front. She'd fix it for her later.

"How is he?"

Doris's loosely braided silver hair frayed out around her face. The last time Peachy had seen her looking so weary was when she'd been in hospital. The woman wore her heart on her sleeve and took in the emotions and pains of others so easily. Of course, she would have done anything for her only daughter. Even sell forgeries to pay the hospital bills.

"He had triple bypass surgery last night. The docs said they expect a complete recovery, but that it could be slow going."

"I'm so sorry, Mum." She tugged a chair over to sit beside her. "He means a lot to you, doesn't he?"

"He does, darling." She patted Peachy's hand. The gentle swoosh of some medical device was audible from behind the bed. "Heinrich and I have been... Well, I'm sure you've intuited that we have a thing."

"I've suspected."

"He's not a boyfriend, more like a lover. But a permanent one, if that makes sense."

It could only make sense in Doris Cohen's life. "I understand, Mum. It's nice to have a companion."

"I love him. But how are you? You didn't get the final painting?"

"It was pulled from auction. I'm not sure why. And I wasn't able to speak to Mr. Lawrence."

She could have. She just hadn't the fortitude to stand before Krew after she'd accused him of not being on her side. A side that was in no way, shape or form a side the man could ever take. He was upright, honest and had a sterling reputation. The last thing she'd want to do was tarnish it.

"Don't worry about it, Mum. I'll find a way to pay you back for the hospital bills. If you would have told me sooner—"

"I don't need repayment, darling. Those are taken care of and in the past. That's not why I wanted those paintings off the market, and you know that. I just don't believe I'd be able to pull off prison stripes."

"Oh, Mum." Peachy hugged her.

"Does your Mr. Lawrence know? Did you tell him?"

Peachy didn't want to lie to her mother but she should have never let another person in on the secret. Especially one who had a penchant for doing the right thing when it came to art.

"You did." Doris nodded. "You have fallen in love."

"I haven't—"

Her mum lifted her chin, eyeing her with that sparkle that told Peachy she knew her daughter's heart better than even she did at times. And besides, she may have actually manifested him into her life.

"I needed a confidant. I'm sorry. I just… This is too much, Mum. It's a huge secret to keep."

"You owe me, darling. We Cohen women are strong. At the very least, you can do this for me."

It was a rare sighting of the other side of Doris Cohen, her cold lack of empathy and determination to get her way. Or perhaps it was a mother's instinctive need to protect her child at all costs.

"When will he be in condition to go home?" she asked of Heinrich.

"I don't know. Probably weeks."

"Someone will have to oversee the gallery while he's away. I'll do that."

"Of course you will. Heinrich would expect it."

So many who expected her to do their bidding. It was tiring. Defeating. Peachy felt as though she had given all she could with no return. She could never sell those paintings, and would Heinrich even acknowledge, let alone honor, their agreement to raise her commissions?

"I'm going home to relax. I came here straight from Heathrow. I'll text you later?"

"Of course. Do let me know when you've secured *Dance*."

Peachy stood and wandered to the door, unwilling to reply that she'd be right on that task. Her mother could bear to share some of the worry over this fiasco. Yes, even with her lover lying in the hospital.

* * *

Once home, Krew set the unwrapped painting by the brick wall between the two floor-to-ceiling windows that looked over central London. It was midnight. A crescent moon sat high in the sky above Big Ben, mimicking the curve of the lighted clock face. The flight home had been turbulent. And Peachy had not been sitting beside him. A text inquiring where she had gotten to hadn't been answered.

He tugged off his tie, tossed it to the floor and wandered to the liquor cabinet in search of something to ease the stress. There, at the top, sat a sixty-thousand-dollar bottle of single malt Scottish whisky, purchased from the maker whose family had been distilling the liquor for centuries. It had been a goal when he was a teenager for Krew to purchase the whisky. Something his father would admire him for. Yet he'd still not told him he owned it.

Byron Lawrence had always kept his prized bottle of whisky high on a shelf in their family room. When he was little, Krew would watch his dad dust the thick glass bottle. Say things to it. Pat it. He'd doted on that damn bottle more than on his son. And Krew had known then that it had meant more to his dad than he did. He'd always known his father's love was conditional.

Byron Lawrence was distracted by things and not sentiments.

Now, as he held the bottle, unopened, he couldn't quite touch that sense of victory he'd experienced when first purchasing it. The feeling he'd bested his dad. *Look! I too can own a ridiculous bottle of alcohol that I keep on my shelf and dust.*

Krew couldn't imagine having a child and showing an inanimate object more love.

Setting the bottle on the kitchen counter, he leaned his palms on the cold marble and bowed his head. So much he'd lost in the past days. But nothing hurt more than watching Peachy walk away from him after the auction. He'd give a thousand bottles of expensive whisky to see her walk back into his arms.

He didn't want to value *things*. Nor did he want to run from romance. From love. As the nuns had told her, people were indeed here on earth to love and be loved. And it was time he started believing that as much as Peachy did. He only needed her. In his arms. In his life. He could be there for her.

And yet, he had not been there for her at the auction when she'd likely most needed his support. Once again, he had failed a woman he cared about.

He smiled a little. Her dreams of country living had permeated his being. He imagined sharing that dream alongside her.

Peachy hadn't purposely lured him into this mess. She hadn't even known about the forgeries. Her mum had sold them to Byron to pay for her daughter's medical bills and he could imagine it had felt like the only possible way at the time. Not necessarily right but something she could do to get by. Peachy had described her mother as bohemian, a beguiler. She may have thought the fakes were so good they'd never be discovered.

And they had not. Krew had walked by those paintings many times, looked at them, studied the *Melancholy*, for heaven's sake. He'd never noticed anything off.

Of course, he hadn't been looking at them with a trained eye at the time. And any forgery could slip by the most skilled dealer if that person were not intentionally looking for a fake.

Truly, Peachy was not to blame in any of this mess. Her only guilt was in opening his heart and stepping inside with her natural sexy confidence.

Straightening, Krew knew he had to make a bold step. He must protect all those he cared about. And he would.

He peeled the red sealing wax from the whisky bottle and loosened the cap. It smelled…like the best whisky he'd ever known. Like something Byron would admire and attend to without concern for those things in life that were real, honest and, yes, family.

Tilting it over the sink, he watched as the golden liquid glugged out and down the drain. He didn't even wince. It didn't matter any longer that he had the upper hand over some silly competition he'd created between him and his dad.

What did matter was that Krew Lawrence was going to stand up for the one he cared about.

Wandering over to the packaged painting, he carefully peeled away the brown paper to reveal the canvas. And when he stepped back, he saw what had been evident, for the first time, in the auction house.

Now he realized why, during that first auction, he'd thought Peachy looked so familiar.

Krew shook his head and chuckled. "Oh, Doris, I do love you."

CHAPTER TWENTY-TWO

THE NEXT MORNING Krew went over things with the crew as they filmed *Jar and Flower*. They'd taped him talking to the forensics scientist, getting a short, easily digestible lesson on how they took microscopic flakes of paint and canvas from the work and used radiocarbon dating to determine age. The Daves then followed the scientist to the room where a high-resolution digital scanner waited.

Krew gestured he'd be right in. He wondered now if he should buy *Melancholy* and *The Deluge* from Peachy so he could have them analyzed as well. But really, Peachy had already confirmed they were forgeries. Today's filming was merely for the benefit of the show. He knew what the results would ultimately show.

And he guessed Hammerstill would never sell. The paintings would be burned. End of story. Hammerstill would be out hundreds of thousands for that trouble.

Krew could step in and lessen the financial burden. If he wanted to. He didn't owe Heinrich a thing. Not a single pence. But that the old man had employed Peachy, and her mother did mean something.

His phone pinged with a text from Peachy saying she wanted to call but wasn't sure he wanted to hear from her. Shaking his head, he pressed her number and she answered on the first ring.

"I'm sorry I had to leave Andalusia so quickly. It's Heinrich. He's had a triple bypass," she said, followed by a heavy sigh. "He won't be able to work any longer. He's said he wants to begin paperwork to hand the gallery ownership to me."

"That's remarkable." But he realized the enthusiasm was not appropriate. The old man had had a heart attack. "I'm so sorry about Heinrich."

"Thank you. I, uh, have been thinking about the forgeries we've purchased. And there is still the issue of the painting you won. *Jar and Flower* must never be resold or placed in a museum. But you are aware of that, I'm sure."

"Yes, the painting will never be placed before the public again. But we will use it for a show. I don't want to talk about that right now. Can we meet? I want to see you, Peach. Come to my place?"

"I can stop by this evening," she said.

* * *

He'd called her Peach. She wanted to cry. To believe that she could really have him in her life. To know that their future had not been destroyed by some hippie named Dickie who had thought to help out a woman who had only been trying to survive and take care of her daughter.

Nervous about seeing Krew, Peachy paid attention to her hair, her dress, her shoes. Her lipstick seemed to be the wrong tone so she switched it up for something a little redder. That went well with the red dress. Polka dots as usual. She liked them. They were fun.

But did she appear too flirty, too much the toss-aside woman for what could be the we-can't-do-this-anymore talk they might have? Krew had every right to walk away from what they'd started. She was involved in a ridiculous forgery scheme. Not by choice. But…whew!

Lift your chin, she coached as she headed out to catch an Uber. *Get through this night and then move forward tomorrow.*

If tomorrow didn't have Krew in it she would be devastated. No little house in the country would matter if the one person she cared about most were not in her life to share it with.

The driver stopped before Krew's building and she got out. Taking in the building front, she tilted her head all the way back. His penthouse overlooked the Thames and the city center. Thanks to his success, the man could have anything he desired. And for a moment, she'd thought to be included in those desires.

She touched the scarf she'd tied about her neck. She could do this.

The lift moved so rapidly she clutched her cane and placed the other hand to the wall for stability. When the doors opened, she held her finger on the open button and took a moment to regain her equilibrium.

Before she could even knock on Krew's door it opened and his smile grabbed her nerves by the scruff and flicked them away. He took her hand and led her inside. The cool brick-and-wood exterior was so masculine. Perfectly him. With a glance over her shoulder, she eyed the Matisse. The country scene seemed a little too sprightly for the dread that lingered just below her throat.

He kissed her on the cheek. Not the mouth. Did that mean…? Her nerves sat up from where he'd tossed them and decided to stick around for a while.

"How's Heinrich?" He gestured she sit on one of the leather sofas.

She went to the sofa and sat. "Mum is there with him. He'll need some time for recovery."

"And he's asked you to take his place. That's what you wanted, right?"

She leaned against the back of the sofa, setting her cane aside. The floor-to-ceiling windows brightened the room filled with brick, leather and dark woods. Between the two windows sat a canvas covered with a sheet. She was curious about it, but more curious about their relationship right now.

"Taking on a managerial position will help me get closer to that country cottage," she said. They needed to move beyond polite chat before those nerves of hers did a dance about her system. "What will you do with *Jar and Flower*?"

"I'll be using it as a teaching example for the show. Forensics just confirmed it was painted less than a decade ago."

"Which I've already explained to you. But how can you put it on the show without explaining provenance, which will trace it back to the Hammerstill Gallery?"

He shifted, propping an elbow on the table, and faced her. For a man so uptight and astute his posture was downright casual and open. And then she realized he wore a shirt unbuttoned at the top. And no tie!

"Wait." She leaned forward and tapped the base of his neck, then tugged at the shirt collar.

"Right?" His smile was so broad now she knew something had changed significantly in Krew Lawrence. Maybe he was sick? He was certainly not feeling his normal self. "This is the one with the button you sewed on for me. I cherish it. And I can do casual, Peach."

He'd called her Peach. And he cherished the shirt. That lifted her shoulders.

"I like you casual," she said. "But it'll take some getting used to. I have no way to judge your mood without the tie."

"My shield?"

She nodded. "No need for a protective shield today?"

"Not at all. As for the ink wash, I understand that the gallery could be implicated in a crime and… I don't want to do that to the old man. He's having a tough time of it as it is. And with the forger dead there's no one to prosecute. Save, well… Anyway, I spoke to Byron. He's upset about the loss, but also unwilling to take forgeries back into his home. I intend to cover his losses. Which means there's really no need to pursue legal action. I've discussed it with my producer and he understands as well. We'll use the painting but it's not necessary to divulge the details as to names and locations of any galleries or owners' hands it has passed through."

"Really? That would mean so much if you can do that. But you shouldn't have to pay your dad for the loss."

"It's best for us both. Erases any sense of monetary obligation I may feel toward him. Keeps the old man happy. Besides, I'm doing this mostly for you, Peach."

"You're doing this for *me*?"

"Of course." He slid closer and took her hand. "I decided you should be the winner of this round. And really, it's not going to affect me or The Art Guys if we use this as a teaching moment on the show. The editing team has already remarked that they are going to make it look as though I was specifically on a quest for a forged work. I think it'll work. Though they still insist on using our interactions. Are you good with that?"

"I am. As you've said, there was nothing untoward between us. At least, not that was filmed. But what about the two works I've won? Those are forgeries. And as far as I know, Heinrich wanted them burned."

"Then we'll burn them."

"As simple as that?"

"Of course, but not until you allow me to buy them from you first. Heinrich won't be out any money that way."

"Why be so kind to a man who has been the thorn in The Art Guys' sides for years?"

"I'm not vindictive," he said. "Not like…" He sighed. "Byron's ex-wife did a mean thing. It was calculated and cruel. But Byron going after the paintings was just as selfish in different ways, not to mention a little childish. He's an art hoarder. He doesn't buy things to admire and cherish—he buys them for status and boasting rights. 'I have the most and you don't,' that sort of thing. I'm not like that. I don't need to prove I'm better by owning more. Nor do I need to bring another man, like Hammerstill, down because it'll make me appear the better. That's not being better."

Peachy leaned forward and he bumped foreheads with her. For a moment they sat there, taking it in. Skin against skin. He was a true gentleman. Her calm warrior of the shielded ties. She could love him.

She did love him.

"If your mum will verify that only three forgeries were sold to my father, I'll trust her," he said. "I'll want to speak to her, of course."

"She will. I'll make sure of it. She promised me there were only the three."

"So, that leaves the final one on your list. *Dance.*"

"Mum tells me it's not a fake."

"Yes, I have determined that."

"You have?"

He nodded to the windows where the sheet covered a canvas. "Let me show you."

He took her hand as she stood. "You got it? I thought it had been pulled from the auction."

"Another sneaky move on Claudia's part. I spoke to the auction manager, explained the situation and…offered him double what Claudia was hoping to get for it. She immediately accepted the offer. Come take a look."

As they stood before the sheet-covered canvas, Krew took both her hands. "Before I show you this, I want you to know something. You've changed me, Peach. And I don't want to go back to what I was."

"You are a fine man, Krew. You don't need to change anything."

"But I do. You've taught me about love. How it can be so many things. That I am worthy of it. You've altered my heart. Tugged away my protective shield."

"I adore your various tie knots. It's the best way to read you."

"It's a language only you know." He slid his hand along her jaw and stroked her cheek. "Peachy, I love you."

A feeling no master could ever do justice with paints or inks trilled through her insides, stirred in her belly and burst through her being. Clutching Krew's unbuttoned shirt, she said, "I love you too. But with the secrets, I…didn't know if we'd have a chance."

"We do. If you want us to."

"You're the best thing to come into my life, darling."

"Good, because I only want the best for you. And… I want to help your dreams come true. This might be fast, but I want to help you look for land. Maybe a place we could share together?"

That *was* fast, but… She thought of her vision board in her tiny studio apartment. Krew's photo had been close to center, right beside the cottage photo.

"Sounds like the dream I've been chasing for years."

He pulled her close and they swayed there for a while. Dancing the only way she could. In the arms of the man she loved.

"You'll always have dance," he whispered. "Just like this."

"Only with you. Forever."

With a kiss to the crown of her head, Krew stepped over to the covered canvas. "Take a look at *Dance*." He pulled the sheet from the painting and Peachy approached it. "Your mum is the artist, yes?"

"Yes," she said quietly. There was no doubt. The brightly colored abstract swirls were undeniably Doris's unique style.

"And the model?"

Peachy touched her lips. The abstract clearly

showed a female dancer and though her face was blurred it was apparent she had freckles. And dark hair pulled back. The dress was a polka dot *bata de cola*, a traditional flamenco dress, in Peachy's favorite shades of red and pink. Was it really…?

"Me?"

Krew wrapped his arms around her waist. "This painting hung in the hallway at my parents' home. On the occasions I'd visit Byron, I used to sit on the sofa, so far away, and notice that viewing it from a distance the dancer looked so clear. And I remember when I first saw you at auction you looked familiar. That is you, Peach. And this painting, I believe, is a love letter from your mother to you."

Catching her breath, Peachy felt a tear begin to spill down her cheek. It was lovely. And if Doris had painted it to make money to cover her bills it had to have been created about the time she'd lost her dream of dancing. Of studying flamenco in Andalusia. Truly, this was a mother's tribute to her daughter.

"I don't want to give it back to her," Krew said. "I'd like to keep it. Place it on the wall where the Matisse is."

"You'd trade a Matisse for a Doris Cohen?"

"In a heartbeat. But I won't trade you for the world, Peach."

EPILOGUE

Six months later...

JOSS AND GINNY'S wedding reception was held in a flower-festooned gazebo in the least-expected place for a wedding, Transylvania. The guest list was small, private, but perfect for the ceremony held before the lake. Having met Ginny a few times previously when the three Art Guys had gathered with their significant others, Peachy had grown to adore her. She was giggly, fun and smart, and the bright yellow and orange flowers appliquéd on her white dress matched her personality. She and Joss had fallen in love while on a job to appraise a dusty old library in Transylvania and everyone was now jokingly calling her Mrs. Brawn, and she loved it.

Sipping champagne and taking in the fresh air tinted with the smell of pine needles and the sound of vibrant dance music, Peachy looked around for her Mr. Brain. Well, The Brain. She'd moved into his penthouse two months earlier, after four months of dating. Finally, she had found real love.

They'd looked at a few different plots for sale outside Bath. It was a bit farther from London than Krew had planned on, but he loved the area, as did she. Krew was all in for building a little cottage and having goats. She still wasn't so sure about the goats, but she did like to indulge her lover.

Bumped from behind, she turned to find Krew's back to her. He was rocking gently…

"Oh, my gosh." She turned around before him. "Is that…? Darling, what are you holding?"

Her handsome lover had chosen the Desiderata tie knot to go with his groomsman attire this evening. He was truly her heart's desire.

"This," he said plainly, "is a baby. They are common throughout the entire world. A miniature version of human."

What a joker! "Fair enough." It was Maeve and Asher's daughter. Peachy had been eyeballing the tyke all evening. At two months she was so tiny and adorable.

"Smell her head," Krew offered, lifting the baby to her nose.

Peachy pressed her nose to the baby's tuft of thick black hair. "Mmm, smells like…"

"Heaven?"

"And like sweets and your favorite memory."

"Right?" He hugged the baby and continued rocking. "I like her."

"Oh dear." Maeve suddenly intruded, reaching for the baby. "That's where Scarlet got to. It's time for your bottle, love." Then she said to Krew, "I'm not even going to ask what you're doing with my delicious little nugget. I know she's been circulating."

Both Peachy and Krew laughed as Maeve wandered off, bouncing Scarlet gently.

Krew slipped his hand into hers. "Babies are nice."

They'd not discussed children, how they felt about them or if they would like to have them in their future. If they even moved toward that future. But Krew's simple statement blossomed in Peachy's heart and she tilted her head to his shoulder. "They are. I'd like one."

He nodded. "Yeah? Me too."

With a whistle, the crowd settled. On the dais under the floral arch, the bride stepped up and swung her bouquet. "Time to toss the bouquet!"

"I'm out of here." Krew gave Peachy a nudge as he quickly left the dance floor.

Leaning onto her cane to keep from toppling, Peachy looked for a quick exit as well, but a half circle of women had formed, and for some reason she stood in the middle. She wasn't one for such theatrics. But the bouquet, brimming with white roses and eucalyptus, was beautiful. What was it they said about the woman who caught the bouquet—she would be the next to marry?

"Worth a try," she whispered. Though Krew's fast escape did not bode well for that future.

Ginny raised the bouquet, turned her back to the crowd and gave it a toss.

And…without stepping forward, Peachy suddenly felt the heavy bouquet of flowers land against her chest. She caught it with one hand. Cheers erupted around her. The fragrance seeped upward like expensive perfume. So gorgeous. Did that mean…?

Turning to look for her man, she startled to find Krew standing right behind her.

"Krew?"

"Peach."

When he went down on one knee, Peachy caught a gasp at the back of her throat. This was…so unexpected. And yet, he held up a ring and she could barely hear him speak as the crowd again clapped and cheered.

"You've taught me that love is all a person needs. I love you, Peach. Marry me!" he shouted so she could hear.

She nodded. "Yes!"

Krew slipped the ring onto her finger. He kissed her to renewed applause. Together they would touch their dreams.

* * * * *

Get up to 4 Free Books!

We'll send you 2 free books from each series you try PLUS a free Mystery Gift.

FREE
Value Over
$25

Both the **Harlequin® Historical** and **Harlequin® Romance** series feature compelling novels filled with emotion and simmering romance.